WARPED GALAXIES

WAR OF THE

ORKS

WARHAMMER ADVENTURES

STORIES FROM THE FAR FUTURE

WARPED GALAXIES

WARHAMMER ADVENTURES

STORIES IN AN AGE OF FANTASY

REALM QUEST

WARHAMMER™
ADVENTURES
STORIES FROM THE FAR FUTURE

WARPED GALAXIES

WAR OF THE

ORKS

CAVAN SCOTT

WARHAMMER ADVENTURES

First published in Great Britain in 2020 by
Warhammer Publishing,
Willow Road,
Nottingham, NG7 2WS, UK.

10 9 8 7 6 5 4 3 2 1

Produced by Games Workshop in Nottingham.
Cover illustration by Cole Marchetti.
Internal illustrations by Magnus Norén & Cole Marchetti.

A CIP record for this book is available from the British Library.

ISBN 13: 978 1 78193 962 8

This is a work of fiction. All the characters and events portrayed
in this book are fictional, and any resemblance to real people or
incidents is purely coincidental.

See Warhammer Adventures on the internet at

warhammeradventures.com

Find out more about Games Workshop and the worlds of
Warhammer 40,000 and Warhammer Age of Sigmar at

games-workshop.com

Printed and bound by CPI Group (UK) Ltd, Croydon, CR0 4YY

For Connie.

Contents

The Imperium
of the Far Future

Life in the 41st millennium is hard.
Ruled by the Emperor of Mankind
from his Golden Throne on Terra,
humans have spread across the
galaxy, inhabiting millions of planets.
They have achieved so much, from
space travel to robotics, and yet
billions live in fear. The universe
seems a dangerous place, teeming
with alien horrors and dark powers.
But it is also a place bristling with
adventure and wonder, where battles
are won and heroes are forged.

CHAPTER ONE

Aftermath

Hinterland Outpost was a wreck. Smouldering cruisers littered the landing bay, once-precious cargo scattered among the wounded and dying. Inquisitor Jeremias marched up to a medic who was doing her best to tend to a wounded docker. One glance told the inquisitor that the injured man wasn't long for this world. Jeremias had experienced many battlefields and knew a lost cause when he saw one.

'What happened here?' he asked, and the medic jumped at the unexpected question. She turned, her eyes widening

as she took in Jeremias's Inquisitorial rosette and the servo-skull floating at his epauletted shoulder.

'There was an attack,' she said, turning back to her patient. 'The Tau.'

Jeremias's mouth curled into a snarl. 'The Upstart Empire. Here. And you fought them off?'

The woman didn't answer.

'Well?'

She glared up at him. 'Look, I'll answer your questions, but only after I've treated this man. His wounds are serious.'

'His wounds were terminal,' Jeremias corrected her.

She looked back to the docker and sighed. The man had gone.

Jeremias watched as she pulled out a cracked data-slate and recorded his time of death. The woman was impressive. Not many citizens would stand up to an inquisitor, even in such grave situations. She had spirit.

The medic closed the man's unseeing eyes and stood to address Jeremias. 'Yes,' she said, wiping blood from her hands onto a rag that looked decidedly unsanitary. 'We fought back, for all the good it did us. The power grid is on its last legs, and most of the station's occupants are dead or dying.'

'But you didn't fall to the xenos scum,' Jeremias pointed out. 'Praise the Throne.'

She repeated the oath, although her words were hollow. 'Is that why you're here?' she asked. 'Is the Imperium sending aid?'

He raised an immaculate eyebrow, and

the woman scowled.

'I mean...' she stammered, her expression hardening, 'I realise that's not what you people do...'

'"You people"?'

'The Inquisition. I just thought... seeing what happened here...'

Jeremias looked around the wrecked landing bay. 'Hinterland Outpost has long been a cesspool of villainy and heresy, operating outside the Emperor's law. It is good that you fought back against the Tau, but even if supplying aid was within my duties, I see little worth saving.'

Her mouth dropped open. 'How can you say that? People are dying here. *Humans* are dying here.'

His eyes paused on a nearby corpse. It was a Kroot, its alien tongue lolling from a beaked mouth. 'Was that one of the Tau's retinue?'

She glanced at the fallen alien. 'No. That was Skrann. He worked here, unloading cargo. He was a decent sort.'

Jeremias saw her flinch at her own words, and for good reason.

'Xenos working alongside humans,' Jeremias said, his tone judgemental. 'And you don't see a problem in that?'

'All I meant was—'

He raised a gloved hand to stop her. 'I know what you meant, but the argument is moot. There's an old Terran saying — "You dug your trench, you sleep in it." This is your problem, not the Imperium's.'

'So if you're not here to help...?' The medic left the question hanging. Her insolence was beginning to grate.

'I am looking for survivors of a recent tragedy in the Segmentum Pacificus. Three children. A girl and two boys.'

Her eyebrows shot up. 'Segmentum Pacificus? But that's—'

'A long way from here — yes, yes it is. I have reason to believe that they travelled here.'

The medic's eyes narrowed. 'To Hinterland. Why? *How?*'

11

'It is forbidden to question an inquisitor's methods,' snapped Corlak, Jeremias's loyal servo-skull.

He waved away his familiar's outrage. 'Have you seen them?' he asked the woman.

The medic laughed bitterly. 'Have I seen children? On Hinterland? I tell you what I've seen. Bodies. Lots and lots of bodies. And that number increases with every hour. Our medical supplies were destroyed in the attack. I have nothing to work with. And you're asking me about *children*?'

This was getting him nowhere. He turned away, looking for someone else to question.

'No... wait. *Please.*'

A hand grabbed his arm and pulled him back. The woman had actually touched him! He swung around, pushing her away. She stumbled, falling onto the body of the man she had tried to save.

'That was your last warning,' he

barked at her. 'I suggest you stay down.'

'I'm sorry...' the medic said, visibly shaking. 'I just... all this... it's too much. The Emperor...'

'The Emperor will protect you from darkness,' he interrupted. 'Now go about your work.'

She nodded and started picking up her supplies. Jeremias watched her for a moment. Was she right? Should he help? *Could he?* No. This was not his mission.

He turned, aware of Grimm – his cyber-mastiff – watching from the ramp of his ship. The hound looked ready to charge, to attack the woman for daring to touch him. The inquisitor raised a hand and the mechanical beast stalked back up the ramp, cybernetic eyes glowing red.

She had learned her lesson. She would do as he said, helping the survivors of the battle. She had her duties... and Jeremias had his.

The inquisitor looked around. The tech-savants had vanished, no doubt spooked by the altercation. Jeremias sighed. He would have to venture deeper into the station to find someone to question. The children had come here. Of that, the visions had been clear.

'Looking for the kiddies, are you?'

The voice was gruff, unrefined. Jeremias turned to see a goat-faced Beastman sitting beneath the wreck of a skimmer. The abhuman smiled, showing uneven brown teeth. 'I can tell you about the kids, if you can get me off this dump.'

Jeremias's eyes narrowed. 'I'm listening...'

CHAPTER TWO

The Emperor's Seat

On the flight deck of the *Profiteer*, all eyes were on Talen Stormweaver. The ship was the pride and joy of Harleen Amity, rogue trader and adventurer. As the son of an Imperial Guard drillmaster, Talen had been brought up on tales of the Astra Militarum. He had been taught about duty and honour, about the glory of dying in the Emperor's service. He'd never liked the sound of that, especially the last bit. But rogue traders? They were different. Rogue traders went where they wanted. Rogue traders answered to no one.

When his brother went off to war,

Talen vowed never to take orders. That hadn't always worked, but now he was free. Okay, he was running scared with a bunch of misfits and refugees, but for the first time in his life no one was telling him what to do.

No one except Zelia Lor, of course. Even though she was a year younger than him, she clearly thought she was in charge. Granted, the competition wasn't great. The rest of the group was made up of Mekki, a Martian who'd rather spend time tinkering with machines than dealing with people; Meshwing, the Martian's skittish servo-sprite; an ape-like Jokaero that everyone except for Mekki called Fleapit; and a mindless servitor who was nicknamed Grunt. Captain Amity had been promised a small fortune if she helped them find Zelia's mum, so even the rogue trader listened to the girl.

For now at least.

'So?' Zelia asked. 'What did Karter say?'

They had just come from Hinterland Outpost, a trading post near Tau space where they'd met with Karter, an unscrupulous cartographer. Talen had tricked the crook into giving them the location of the Emperor's Seat, the planet where Zelia believed she would be reunited with her mother.

The only problem was that Karter had given him not one but *three* possible locations.

'Well,' Talen said, 'there's Terra for a start.'

'Where the Emperor literally sits upon his Throne,' Zelia said. 'We've already discounted that.'

'Correct,' Mekki agreed. Meshwing buzzed around the Martian's bald head before settling on his narrow shoulders. 'Getting to the Throneworld would be problematic.'

'For all of us,' Amity chipped in.

'So...' Zelia prompted, looking expectantly at Talen.

'So, Karter had heard of two other

possible locations. The first is Weald, a forest world on the edge of the Eastern Fringe.'

The words were barely out of his mouth before Mekki had turned to the *Profiteer*'s cogitator and was accessing the ship's extensive star charts. A hololith of a vibrant green planet appeared in the middle of the flight deck.

'And what's the other?' Zelia asked.

'Pastoria.'

Again, Mekki searched the databank, this time linking the haptic connectors on his fingers to the cogitator's access ports. 'I can find no planet with that name,' he reported. 'You must be mistaken, Talen Stormweaver.'

'Maybe not,' Amity cut in. 'Try the Legends of the Emperor.'

Mekki raised a faint eyebrow. 'I am sorry?'

The rogue trader shrugged. 'An old scroll from my family's archives. It's probably nonsense, of course, little more than fairy tales – but it's been passed down from generation to generation.'

Mekki resumed his search and this time nodded excitedly. 'Yes. Pastoria is mentioned.' His grey eyes flickered as he read the ancient text scrolling up the screen. 'According to the scribe, the Emperor's company visited the planet after a particularly brutal battle...'

'Against whom?' Zelia asked.

Mekki shrugged. 'It does not say, only that the Emperor "rested among the swaying crops of Pastoria".'

'But where is it?' Zelia asked.

'There are no coordinates.'

'But there are clues,' Talen said. 'The passage mentioned crops. Could be a – what do you call it? A farm planet.'

'An *agri* world,' Zelia said. 'But without any galactic coordinates we don't even know if it exists. It might be just a story.'

Talen pointed at the hololith of Weald. 'What about this place, then?'

Amity checked her console. 'The records

are sketchy. It's said to be mainly covered in forests, no known life forms.'

'But there *is* a reference to it in the legends,' Mekki cut in, twisting his haptic implants in the sockets. 'It is believed that a battle was waged there, long ago.'

'Between who?' Zelia asked.

Mekki shook his head. 'I do not know, but a tribute was raised to the Emperor afterwards. A monument.'

'Can we see it?' Talen asked.

More hololiths fizzed into life. They showed stained-glass windows, each displaying a different scene.

'These are from a temple on Terra,' Mekki explained.

Zelia pointed at stylised figures in the glass, clad head to foot in blue power armour. 'Those are Space Marines.'

Mekki nodded. 'Ultramarines. After the battle, they carved an image of the Emperor into a mountainside.'

Mekki gave his implants another twist and more stained-glass panels appeared. The first showed a mountain, Ultramarines gunships buzzing around its peak. The image shifted, and now the gunships were firing on the mountainside, their lasers slicing into the rock.

Another shift and a gigantic statue stood where the mountain had been, a towering effigy of the Emperor sitting on his Throne.

Talen's mouth dropped open. 'Surely that can't be real? Gunships couldn't have done all that, could they? It has to be a myth.'

'The gunships *do* seem unlikely,' Amity acknowledged, 'but, in my experience, Ultramarines are capable of some pretty incredible things. Maybe they carved it by hand?'

'That would take some doing,' Zelia said.

'A task worthy of a Space Marine, then.' Amity swivelled her chair to face Mekki. 'Are there any images of the statue itself?'

The Martian checked and the stained glass disappeared to be replaced with a hololith of the gigantic sculpture.

Talen couldn't get his head around it. The effort needed to reshape an entire mountainside was mind-boggling. He knew that Space Marines were dedicated, but this... this was on a different level.

'That *has* to be the Emperor's Seat,' Zelia said, gazing at the statue. The effigy stared back, an imperious look on its face, the jawline quite literally chiselled. It was hard to imagine what it would be like to see this in real life, to stand in the trees that clustered around the stone Emperor's feet, looking up at the colossus.

One way or another, they would find out soon enough.

'Captain Amity,' Zelia said, turning to the rogue trader. 'Please set course for Weald. We're going to find my mum.'

Amity fought to keep a smile from her face. 'Remind me to congratulate her for raising such an assertive daughter.' She swivelled around to her controls and grabbed the flight stick. 'Who wants to co-pilot?'

'I will,' Talen said, almost sprinting to her side.

He could feel Mekki glowering at the back of his neck. 'But you have not even flown a skimmer,' the Martian said.

'Then it's about time he learned,' Zelia said, backing him up for once. 'Besides, you and Fleapit have got your Tau battlesuit to play with.'

'I do not play,' Mekki huffed, disconnecting his implants to join the Jokaero, who was already working on the battle armour they'd stolen from the trading post.

His heart beating fast, Talen lowered himself into the co-pilot's seat.

'Okay, kid,' Amity said, smiling at him. 'Let's see what you can do.'

CHAPTER THREE

Weald

Zelia watched through the armourglass viewport as the *Profiteer* dropped into Weald's atmosphere. Talen had taken to the ship's controls like a crotalid to water. She'd even go so far as to say he was a natural. She'd spent her entire life on board a spaceship, helping her mother pilot their star-hopper from one dig to another. Talen, on the other hand, had grown up in the tunnels of an underhive, fighting to survive; yet here he was, hands flitting across the *Profiteer*'s controls as if he belonged in the stars.

The void gave way to brilliant blue as they swooped towards the largest of Weald's vast continents. The records had described the planet as covered in woodland, but the reality was more like dense jungle. A sea of green spread out in all directions, the rainforest's canopy thick with leaves.

'Have you found the statue?' Amity asked.

A look of panic flashed over Talen's face. He was trying to match ancient maps Amity had found in the databank to the landscape below. Helping fly a ship had been one thing, but reading holo-maps was another. Zelia knew that Talen wouldn't want to admit that he was struggling. Talen was desperate to impress the captain, and maybe even had a slight crush on the woman. That would explain the way he blushed every time she spoke to him.

Zelia leant in and subtly tapped the display, winking at Talen. He grinned as the navigation systems locked onto the new readings.

'We have map coordinates,' he reported.

'Excellent work,' Amity said, pretending that she hadn't seen Zelia lend a hand. 'Patch them into the navi-cog like I showed you.'

Talen completed the task with a flourish and Amity banked the ship towards their new destination.

'Is that it?' Zelia asked, pointing at a crag in the distance.

Talen peered through the viewport and then brought up a small hololith of the statue the Ultramarines had carved. 'I'm not sure. It's not the same shape, is it?'

Amity pushed the ship on. Talen was right. The Space Marines' tribute had been resplendent, the Emperor sitting in full power armour, a golden wreath around his head. The peak ahead was irregular; crumbling.

They roared on, and Zelia realised that yes, it *was* the same monument.

The gigantic pauldrons were there, as were the enormous arms resting on the carved throne, but the millennia had taken their toll on the effigy. Half the Emperor's once mighty face was missing, his wreath of office crumbled away. As Amity brought them nearer, they could see vegetation springing from deep fissures running across the statue's pocked chest-plate. The entire thing looked as if it was ready to tumble to the ground, but even in such a decrepit state, the sheer scale was staggering. From an early age, humans were taught that the Eternal Emperor was a colossus who towered over the galaxy, but to see his image looming over the jungle made her head spin.

The Ultramarines had known what they were doing.

'Incoming!'

Zelia's head snapped around, Amity's

warning breaking her reverie. She grabbed the back of Talen's chair as the captain threw the *Profiteer* to the side. Something streaked past the viewport, a line of blazing fire, which was followed by an ear-splitting *boom* as it slammed into the Emperor's tribute.

'Was that a missile?' Talen gasped.

'Yes, and it's brought a friend,' Amity said, as a second rocket came screaming up from the trees.

'Are they firing at us?' Zelia asked, hanging onto Talen's chair, but Amity didn't have a chance to answer. The second missile struck the statue, throwing rubble towards them.

'Hold on,' Amity yelled, as chunks of mountain bounced off their hull. She was trying to bring them about when what looked suspiciously like the Emperor's nose ripped through one of the *Profiteer*'s wings.

The ship pinwheeled through the air. Amity swore, firing the retro-thrusters, but it was no good.

'The automatic systems are overloaded. She's not responding.'

'This is why you need a crew!' Zelia snapped.

'Not helping,' Amity shot back as she wrestled with the controls.

'What about me?' Talen asked. 'How can *I* help?'

'Get everyone to the starboard hatch,' Amity ordered. 'You all need to jump.'

Zelia's eyes went wide. 'Out of the ship? Are you *crazy*?'

'Talen!' Amity growled.

The ganger jumped up and pushed Zelia to the back of the flight deck. 'You heard what she said. Come on. You too, Cog-Boy.'

Mekki and Fleapit didn't argue, jumping down from the Tau suit to run from the bridge. They headed to the hatch, Talen only hesitating when he realised he didn't know what starboard meant.

'To the right,' Mekki snapped, taking the lead.

They found the hatch, along with

a set of grav-chutes in a locker next to the door. At any other time Zelia would have breathed a sigh of relief – the chutes were similar to those on her mother's ship, with bulky field generators and twin jets – but there was no time to relax.

The chute was heavy when she pulled it from the peg, but she slipped her arms through the straps before helping Mekki with his.

'You're going to have to take off your backpack.'

The Martian shook his head. 'It contains all my tools.'

Zelia was about to argue, when Fleapit plucked the grav-chute from her hands and started connecting it to Mekki's bulky pack. The Jokaero's retractable fingers blurred as they worked, and by the time he pulled his hands away, the grav-chute was somehow fused to Mekki's pack.

Talen slammed the hatch control, but the door wouldn't open.

'The mechanism must have jammed,' he said, trying to slide the door back manually. It opened a crack to reveal jungle whizzing past below them. The noise was intense, the roar of rushing air drowning out everything.

Well, almost everything...

'*You need to get a move on,*' Amity's voice boomed over the vox. '*I'm looking for a place to land, and when I say land, I mean crash!*'

Talen lost grip and the door slid back. Fleapit shot out a long arm to stop it from closing.

'What about rebreathers?' Zelia called out.

'*The augurs say the atmosphere's breathable,*' Amity responded. '*At least, I think that's what they're saying. Most of the sensors are offline.*'

'That's comforting,' Talen said, taking the strain again. 'I can hold the door open. Go on. I'll be right behind you.'

'Are you sure?' Zelia asked, but he didn't look at her.

'Can't. Hold. It. Much. Longer.'

Mekki stood on the threshold, staring at the trees whipping past beneath them.

'What are you waiting for?' Talen shouted.

'I... I cannot,' Mekki stammered.

'You need to,' Zelia said. 'You'll be fine.'

'But what if the chute does not open?' the Martian asked. 'What if—'

Mekki's sentence was cut short as he was propelled out of the open hatch by a Jokaero hand shoving him in the back.

'Fleapit!' Zelia exclaimed, but the alien only shrugged and jumped himself.

Zelia glanced at Talen, who was gritting his teeth with the effort of holding open the door, the tendons in his neck standing out like cords beneath his skin.

'Just. Go.'

She took a breath and threw herself from the ship. The wind took

her immediately,
whipping her away
from the *Profiteer*.
Plummeting
towards the trees,
she slapped the
button on her
harness and felt
the suspension field
kick in, cocooning
her in a bubble of
anti-gravity. The
twin jets activated,
blue trails of energy
controlling the speed
of her descent.

It was a strange
sensation, dropping
towards the jungle,
the chute's jets
surprisingly quiet
as the *Profiteer*'s
engines bellowed like
a wounded animal
in the distance. She

glanced around. The jets on Fleapit's chute were lit, but Mekki was in freefall, his arms flailing. His chute hadn't deployed. Twisting the control on her harness, Zelia dialled back the jets to drop faster. She shot past Fleapit, catching up with the falling Martian, who was jabbering in binaric as he wrestled with the controls that Fleapit had added to his pack.

'Not that one,' Zelia yelled. 'Hit the red button. The. Red. Button.'

He looked at her, eyes wide with panic. It was no good. He was paralysed with fear.

Twisting her controls, she kicked out, fighting against the jets to push her own gravity field towards Mekki. The bubble swallowed him up, and she grabbed his arm, pulling him in close as she adjusted the anti-grav controls. Her jets whined, adjusting for both their weight.

'It's okay,' she said, as Mekki clung onto her.

'I could not make it work,' he stammered. 'It would not work.'

'Don't worry about it,' she replied, knowing that would be easier said than done. Mekki had failed to operate a piece of equipment. That was unheard of. The Martian would be beating himself up about this for weeks.

'I am sorry, Zelia Lor. I failed.'

'No, you didn't. For all we know Fleapit didn't wire it in properly.'

'That is unlikely.'

'Or it was broken in the first place. You have nothing to apologise about. It's not like any of us have done this before.'

He nodded, but still wouldn't meet her eye, looking down at the rapidly approaching trees.

She looked around. Fleapit was right behind them, the *Profiteer* now on the horizon, smoke billowing from its damaged wing.

But something was wrong. Someone was missing.

Zelia tapped her wrist-vox against her chin, opening a channel. 'Talen, where are you? Did you jump? Repeat – did you jump?'

CHAPTER FOUR

CHAPTER FOUR

Into the Jungle

'What are you doing here?' Amity said as Talen ran back onto the flight deck.

'Someone had to hold the door for the others,' he replied, plonking himself back into the rattling co-pilot's seat.

'You could have taken Grunt,' she said, nodding to the servitor still standing immobile near the Tau battlesuit, seemingly oblivious to the ship's creaking frame.

'Yeah, but then I wouldn't be able to come back and help you, would I?'

Amity snorted, her incredulity barely noticeable above the wail of numerous warning sirens. 'One flying lesson and he thinks he can help me land.'

'You said you were going to crash. How difficult can it be?'

'It's not as easy as it looks, not if you want to walk away in one piece.'

The flight deck shuddered, nearly throwing Talen from his seat.

'Then you better show me,' he said, hanging onto the console.

She sighed, scanning the sea of towering trees in front of them, their leaves a kaleidoscope of reds, greens and purples. 'Look for yourself,' she said. 'We need somewhere to bring her down. Somewhere relatively clear of trees.'

'On a jungle planet?'

'As I said – not easy.'

Talen pointed ahead. 'There!'

She followed his gaze to see patches of clear ground. 'Are those ships?'

The twisted hulls of various star transports rose out of the trees.

'Looks like we're not the only ones to come down in a hurry. Do you reckon it's the refugees from Targian?'

Amity shrugged. 'Your guess is as good as mine. There's no way to tell from up here.' The nose of the ship struck a treetop, broken branches thwacking into the viewport. 'But getting nearer doesn't seem to be a problem. Hang on to something!'

The reverberating boom of the ship striking the ground sent birds scattering from the treetops. Zelia barely had time to wonder if Amity and Talen had made it off the ship before the gravity bubbles smashed through the canopy and they tumbled to the ground, the jets cutting out as they hit the jungle floor. Zelia and Mekki tumbled forwards into a mulch of old leaves and moss, rolling to stop their bones from shattering on impact. Zelia looked up, spitting rotten vegetation from her mouth, and tried her vox again.

'Talen? Please, come in.'

Mekki was already on his feet. 'They may be out of range.'

'If they survived at all,' she replied, regretting the words as soon as they passed her lips. Of course Amity and Talen had survived. The alternative was too terrible to contemplate.

Mekki helped her up, thanking her once again for saving his life.

'You would have done the same for me.'

She brushed herself down and looked around. The thick canopy cast dark shadows over the jungle floor and in the distance she could hear the whirr of insects' wings. Big wings. *Huge* wings. She shivered. The air was damp. She slipped off her jacket, her shirt already drenched in sweat. Glowing midges buzzed around her face like tiny lume-globes. She swatted them away, trying not to think about the diseases their bites might carry. Long ago, her mum had set the *Scriptor* down on Rana, and insisted on spraying the entire crew in bug repellent before leaving the ship. That hadn't stopped Erasmus getting bitten by a blood-beetle and being ill for weeks. Zelia suddenly felt really tired. It wasn't the heat. It was the memory of her mum's partner, who had died protecting them back on the ice planet. That seemed a lifetime ago.

'Where is Flegan-Pala?' Mekki asked, using Fleapit's real name.

They found the Jokaero near a small river, the foul water running thick and fast over rocks which Zelia was sure had fronds that snatched at any passing detritus. Fleapit wasn't paying attention to the water, but was scampering back and forth, his long fingers rummaging through the slimy mud.

'I want a word with you!' Zelia told the alien as she clambered over a fallen trunk that was thick with moss speckled by tiny blinking eyes. 'Mekki's chute didn't open. We need to talk about acceptable safety standards.'

The Jokaero didn't answer but continued to comb the undergrowth with his long fingers.

'What's he looking for?'

Mekki took a step towards the ape. 'Flegan-Pala?'

The alien didn't look up but responded in an agitated stream of clicks and grunts.

Zelia frowned. 'What is it?'

Mekki's face grew even paler as he translated Fleapit's guttural language.

'The Necron Diadem. Flegan-Pala does not have it with him.'

'He *what*?' Zelia couldn't believe what she was hearing. The Diadem was the reason that they'd ended up here in the first place. It was an ancient Necron artefact that Erasmus had discovered on Targian. The lexmechanic had kept it to himself, thinking that he could profit from the metal crown, but the Necrons had descended on the hive world, pulling Targian apart to find their lost treasure. Before he had died, Erasmus had told her to take the Diadem to her mother. Fleapit had been entrusted with looking after the artefact, stashed in the micro-dimension he wore on his back. And now he had lost it?

No. Wait, that wasn't right. They'd thought that Fleapit still had it when he had gone missing on Hinterland but the alien had hidden the Diadem to keep it safe.

'It was on the ship,' she reminded

them. 'That's what Fleapit said. He hid
it on...'

Her voice trailed off.

'On board the *Profiteer*,' Mekki said
gravely.

'Which has just crashed kilometres
away.'

The Jokaero started slapping his palm
against his head, punishing himself.
Zelia and Mekki jumped in, trying to
stop him. They grabbed his arms and
were nearly lifted off their feet. The
Jokaero was ridiculously strong.

'Woah! Stop that!' Zelia told him. 'No
one's blaming you.'

Fleapit shrugged them off and
whistled a retort.

'What did he say?'

'He says that he blames himself,'
Mekki told her. 'And that is all that
matters.'

Zelia rolled her eyes. Having to talk
Mekki out of a panic attack was one
thing, but dealing with a guilt-ridden
Jokaero was definitely another!

She wiped sweat from her forehead. 'Look, no matter what state the ship's in, the Diadem will have survived. It's almost indestructible, remember? It's Amity and Talen that we have to worry about.'

'It'll take more than a little prang to take us down,' said a voice from Zelia's vox.

She grabbed the sleeve of her jacket. The button on her vox had jammed, keeping the channel open. 'Talen? You're okay?'

'Of course we are. What's monkey-breath panicking about?'

Zelia ignored the insulted grunt that came from the affronted Jokaero.

'The Diadem is on the ship.'

'Where?'

She looked at Fleapit and waited for Mekki to translate his response.

'In a special micro-dimension that "no idiot ganger can open", apparently.'

'Charming.'

'You can talk.'

'Well, it's probably in a better state than most of the ship.'

'That bad, eh?'

'Let's just say that Amity isn't exactly happy.'

Zelia could imagine. 'Can you get back in the air?'

'Not without the help of our resident genius and his hairy assistant.'

'Where are you?'

Behind her, the resident genius was checking his wrist-screen. 'I have pinpointed Talen Stormweaver's location.'

'How far away are they?'

'Approximately five point seven three kilometres from our position.'

Zelia shuddered, glancing around at the multicoloured trees. Thick vines draped down from the branches, smothered in thin hairs that bristled whenever they got near. 'That's going to be a long walk through a jungle,' she said, swallowing hard.

'Especially if we encounter wild animals on the way,' Mekki added.

Zelia shot a tight smile at the Martian. 'That helps, thanks.' She spoke into the vox again, trying not to look at the creepy vines. 'We'll be there as soon as we can, Talen. Will you start repairs?'

'Probably. Or we could check out the other crashed ships?'

'The *what?*'

'We noticed them when we came down. It looks like an entire fleet.'

Zelia's voice caught in her throat. 'Did you see the *Scriptor?*'

'We could barely see anything, we were coming down so fast.'

'But it might be the refugee fleet.'

'Maybe... if this is the Emperor's Seat...'

'Go and check,' she snapped before realising how she sounded. 'Please. It'll be a while until we're with you...'

'And if it is the refugees, they might be able to help us with repairs. Good idea. But I warn you, Zel, the ships looked pretty beaten up.'

It was only later that she realised that Talen had shortened her name. Usually she hated that, but somehow it sounded right coming from him.

'I understand... We're setting off now. Zelia, out.' She turned to Mekki, tying her jacket sleeves around her waist like a belt. 'Which direction are they?'

'This way,' Mekki said, pointing ahead. He set off, stepping over an exposed root. 'But you were right – this will take time.'

Zelia trudged after him. 'It's all right for Fleapit. He'll probably swing from the branches or something.'

There was a hum from behind and Zelia turned to see Fleapit rising up from the ground. He'd transformed his grav-chute into a hover-pack while they were otherwise engaged.

She watched him soar above their heads. 'So much for branches. Hey, Fleapit, any chance of you doing that with our chutes?'

She didn't have to ask Mekki to

translate his sharp grunt of a reply.

'Come on, Mekki,' she said, trudging deeper into the trees. 'We'd better get going.'

CHAPTER FIVE

Footprints

The air was sticky as they made slow progress through the jungle towards the *Profiteer*. The heat sapped their strength and their clothes chafed, plastered to their skin by sweat. Before long, Zelia's head was throbbing and she was finding it difficult to put one foot in front of another. She stumbled, tripping over a root and crashing to the floor, the sudden impact sending multicoloured insects scuttling away from the mulch. It was all she could do to push herself up again.

'You need water,' Mekki said,

stopping to help her. 'You are becoming dehydrated.'

She stood, holding onto Mekki's good arm as the jungle spun around her.

'I wish Talen was with us,' she croaked. 'He always keeps his canteen topped up.'

Mekki looked around. 'Here.' He led her to a thick tree. Large leaves sprouted from short branches near its base, each the size of a dinner plate.

Zelia didn't understand why he was so fascinated by them. 'Yeah, very nice. They're... big.'

'They have to be,' he replied, 'to gather what little light makes it through the canopy. But they are also handy when you are in need of refreshment.'

'I'm not eating leaves.'

'You will not have to.'

He gently pulled one of the branches down to reveal a reservoir of water nestled in the middle of the bowl-like leaf.

She looked at him in wonder. 'How did you know it would be there?'

'The ground is wet,' Mekki said, as if it were obvious. 'That means it rained recently. The leaves catch the water.'

'Should we boil it?'

'If it came from a stream yes, but rainwater will be filtered by clouds and therefore safe to drink.'

'Are you sure?'

'Ninety-nine per cent sure. Unless the leaves are poisonous.'

Her eyes opened wide in alarm.

'I am joking,' he said, his tone as studious as ever. 'While I have never experienced these particular trees, the leaf structure matches hundreds of similar species that are harmless.'

She smiled. 'Ninety-nine per cent of the time?'

Mekki pouted. 'Maybe ninety-eight.'

He folded the leaf so the water poured into Zelia's open mouth. It splashed over her nose and chin, but she didn't care. It tasted wonderful, so pure and fresh, as different to recycled voidship water as she could imagine.

When she had exhausted the supply on the leaf, Mekki found her another, before drinking deeply himself.

'Thank you,' she said, wiping her mouth with the back of her hand. 'How did you learn to do that?'

'When my family were forced...' He stopped, correcting himself. 'When I first left Mars, I... travelled for a short while. I met someone who taught me basic survival skills. I would not be here today if it was not for them.'

Zelia looked deep into Mekki's grey eyes. 'Your family was forced to leave Mars?'

Mekki hesitated, but before he could answer her, Fleapit swooped through the trees, gibbering furiously.

'What is it?' Mekki asked, breaking off to follow the Jokaero as he beckoned them forwards with long orange arms. Zelia held back, finding one last precious drop of water on her leaf.

When she joined them, she could see what had excited Fleapit so much.

The hovering alien had found trees grubbed up and scattered across the jungle floor. It wasn't so much a clearing as a *path*.

'What did this?' she asked, looking at a thick trunk that had been snapped in two as if it was a twig. 'One of the downed ships?'

Mekki glanced around. 'There is no debris or signs of a crash.'

'What about a vehicle, then, driving through the forest?'

Mekki crouched down and examined the ground. 'There are tracks, but they were not caused by a machine.'

She clambered over a log to see for herself, her mouth going dry when she saw what he had found.

Mekki was crouched in the middle of a gigantic footprint. It had three toes, each ending in a curved claw.

Fleapit clicked and grunted above them. There were more footprints

running through the trees. Something
had stampeded through here. Something
huge.

'I wish I could see them from above,'
Mekki said, obviously missing his
ever-attentive servo-sprite, which was
still back on the *Profiteer*. He looked up
at Fleapit. 'Can you lift me up?'

The alien dropped down and hooked
his long arms beneath the Martian's
arms. He hovered back up again, lifting
Mekki from the ground to provide a
bird's-eye view.

'Flegan-Pala is correct,' he shouted down, the holo-cam he wore on his head buzzing slightly as it recorded their surroundings. 'Two sets of footprints running right through the trees.'

'Two?' Zelia asked.

'One larger, one smaller, possibly a creature running on all fours, its front paws slightly smaller than the back.'

Zelia was about to ask if he recognised the tracks when a scream cut through the jungle, high and shrill.

"Eeeeeelp!'

'Did you hear that?' Zelia said, whipping around.

'It was hard to miss,' Mekki replied, jumping down from Fleapit's vantage point.

Zelia had already taken off in the direction of the scream. 'Someone's in trouble. Come on.'

"Elp me. 'Eeeeelp meeee!'

The wails were coming from a

twisted lump of metal that seemed to have dropped out of the sky to land between the trees. To Zelia's untrained eye, it looked like part of a large engine, but with rotor blades and propellers attached to it with no rhyme or reason.

Whoever was shouting was trapped beneath the misshapen contraption.

'Do you think it's one of the refugees?' Zelia asked, as they ran up to the strange machine.

'There is no way to know until we get whoever it is from under the device,' Mekki replied.

'Oo'z that?' the nasally voice replied.

'Someone who can help,' Mekki told them, examining the crude machinery.

Zelia got down on her knees to peer beneath the hunk of steaming metal, but couldn't see anything. 'Are you hurt?'

'Wot do yoo fink? It fell on me 'ead, didn't it? Course I izz 'urt! Get us outta 'ere!'

For a moment, Zelia thought Mekki was about to correct the poor soul's grammar, but instead he tried to lift the engine. She joined in, but it was far too heavy, the hot metal burning their hands.

She looked up at Fleapit, who was keeping his distance. 'Can you help?'

The shaggy alien shook his head, pointing in the direction they had been heading before they'd discovered the giant footprints.

'I know we have to get to the ship,' she said sternly, 'but we can't leave them trapped under that thing.'

Fleapit's jabbered reply made it obvious that he thought they definitely could!

Mekki looked up from the machine. 'Flegan-Pala, please. It is the right thing to do.'

Fleapit hovered for a moment, glaring at the children, before grunting and dropping back down to the ground. Chuntering beneath his breath, he jumped onto the ramshackle device, the heat of the metal not seeming to worry him. He scampered over the machinery, shaking his head as if he had never seen such shoddy workmanship in his life.

Scowling, he removed his grav-chute, indicating for Zelia to do the same. Then he leapt down, removing the anti-grav device he'd attached to Mekki's backpack before clambering back onto the metal monstrosity. He got to work, grunting instructions to Mekki, who helped him connect all three suspension field generators to the machine. When they were done, he jumped back down to the floor and nodded at the Martian. Mekki pressed a button on his wrist-screen and a whine filled the air. As they watched, the heavy device lifted slowly from the ground, nuts and bolts raining down around it.

'That's it, that's it,' encouraged Zelia as it rose into the air. She dropped back to her knees, looking beneath the widening gap. 'You should be able to wriggle...'

The colour drained from her face and she leapt back up.

'We need to go,' she told Mekki. 'We need to go right now!'

Mekki frowned at her, his finger hovering above his controls. 'Why?'

His answer came as a long green arm shot out to grab Zelia's ankle. It was followed by an oversized head, connected to a wiry green body. Wide nostrils flared in a bulbous nose, beady eyes twinkling as a mouth filled with pointed teeth grinned evilly at her.

'Wot 'ave we 'ere?' it wheezed, halfway out of the machine's shadow. 'Humies. 'Orrible, stinkin' humies 'elpin' a grot. Oo-ever 'eard the like?'

Still grinning horribly, the green-skinned creature licked its thin lips and dragged Zelia towards it. She kicked and struggled, her mind racing.

The thing with the pointed teeth and

the vice-like grip was a gretchin, and that could only mean one thing...

CHAPTER SIX

Stick Figures

'Zelia? Can you hear me? Hello?'

On the other side of the jungle, Talen waited for an answer that never came.

'Mekki? Are you there?'

Static hissed from his vox-box. He sighed, clipping it back onto his belt and walking over to join Amity.

'No luck?'

He shook his head. 'I can't get through.'

'They could be out of range, or there's interference from these things.'

The rogue trader slapped the twisted hull of a star transport. The metal was corroded, vines snaking through the flaking armour plates of the once mighty spaceship.

'So much for thinking it was the refugees,' Talen said, looking around.

There were dozens of wrecks dotted around the forest, but it was obvious that they'd been here for a long, long time. Some even had trees growing from inside their superstructures, slimy trunks bursting from the downed ships to reach for the sun.

'Do you reckon they're safe?'

Amity pulled out a handheld auspex and scanned the nearest wreck. 'There's background traces of radiation, but nothing that'll have us growing an extra head... probably.'

Talen watched a long insect with dozens of eyes crawl out of a smashed porthole. 'That's comforting.'

'It might explain what's disrupting the vox signals.' He clambered up the side of the cargo ship, feeling the metal bow beneath his feet. 'Is there anything we could use to patch up the *Profiteer*?'

Amity was trying to prise open an access panel on a rusted skimmer. 'It'll break my heart to use this junk, but maybe, yes – especially if your Jokaero can lend a paw. I've heard he can work wonders.'

'You better believe it, but don't tell him I said so.'

'It'll be our little secret.' The access panel came off in her hands and she threw it aside. The components inside were surprisingly free of moss, although tiny beetles swarmed across the circuitry. Amity brushed them aside with a gloved hand to get a closer look. 'That settles it,' she said, pointing out the serial numbers printed on the circuit board. 'The ships are Imperial, at least originally.'

Talen had reached the top of the cargo ship. 'What do you mean?'

Amity checked on the next downed craft. 'Some of the ships have been... adapted, and crudely too. Parts that were never designed to work together bolted into something new.' She was examining a two-man fighter, its wings stripped away to leave nothing but a cylindrical fuselage which had been subsequently welded to a pair of tank treads. 'But actually, for all its clumsiness, some of the work is actually quite ingenious.'

'I'll take your word for it.' Talen took a step forward and the hull plate beneath his foot creaked, before giving way completely. He cried out as he tumbled into the belly of the ship, crashing to a fungus-strewn floor.

'Talen!'

Amity's voice was muffled by the thick hull plates.

'I'm fine,' he yelled back, prising himself from the ground, light streaming in from the hole in the ceiling. He cursed himself for being so stupid. Hadn't he learned anything since the ice planet and his botched boar hunt?

He spun around as a beamer fired behind him, sending a rusted hatch flying across the darkened space. Amity stepped into the ship, weapon still in hand.

'Careful,' he said. 'You could bring the roof down.'

'Says the boy that fell into a rusty hulk,' she replied, slipping the beamer back into its holster. 'Are you sure you're okay?'

'I'm fine,' he lied, ignoring the pain in his shoulder, which still ached from where he'd dislocated it not long ago. 'What is this place?'

Amity looked around herself. 'A storage hold, although a lot of the central structure has been removed.' She unclipped a brooch from her coat and threw it into the air. Instead of tumbling back to the ground, the four-pointed compass stayed where it was, spinning on its axis like a tiny flying saucer. As it whirled, the star began to glow, flooding the interior of the crashed vessel with a cold blue light.

'Clever gadget,' Talen said. 'Don't let Fleapit get his hands on it.'

'Thanks for the tip.'

Talen paced around the empty space. Amity had been right. The internal walls had been removed, the roof propped up by metal girders that had been welded haphazardly into place.

'It's like Onak's great hall back home,' Talen said, as dust mites danced in the light of the spinning star. 'It used to be a troop carrier before her father got hold of it.'

Amity wasn't listening. She had noticed something on the walls. She pressed a button on her sleeve and the light from the star intensified, reaching the bulkheads.

The walls were covered in crude paintings. Everywhere Talen looked there were hundreds, maybe thousands of stick figures. They were childish in their composition, barely more than blobs for bodies and short stubby lines for the arms and legs. Most were fighting, while others were riding angular machines that belched clouds of black smoke.

'It's a battle,' Talen said, finding a pile of wounded stick figures oozing red paint.

'*Multiple* battles,' Amity agreed. 'But what's that?'

She was pointing at an even bigger blob, this time with sharp triangles for teeth. It looked like a giant mouth on legs, dwarfing the stick figures that clustered around it, weapons drawn.

'It's a sequence,' Amity realised, pressing another button to draw the shining lume-compass nearer. The hovering light followed her as she walked along the hull, revealing each stage of a story. The first picture showed the mouth on legs eating the stick figures, but as they followed the sequence, the stick figures rallied, gathering weapons, chasing the monstrous maw into the trees.

'They're hunting it,' said Talen.

Amity pointed at the next image.
'Without much success.' The creature
had turned on its pursuers, rolling over
them to mash them into the ground. As
they walked around the hull, the story
repeated itself over and over again, the
hunters becoming the hunted, only to
start again.

Talen took a swig from his canteen
and offered it to Amity. 'They didn't
give up, did they?'

The rogue trader took it gratefully.
'Or they were too stupid to realise that
history was repeating.' She passed the
canteen back to him.

'Who do you think painted these?'

Amity ran her fingers across the
flaking metal. 'Natives, maybe.'

'Aliens?'

She squinted, cocking her head to the
side. 'They don't exactly look human.'
She pointed at smaller figures huddled
near the larger ones. 'These could be
children.'

'In a battle?'

She snorted. 'Maybe they are humans after all.'

'What do you mean?'

She shook her head. 'Just thinking aloud.'

Something crunched beneath Talen's boot. Attaching the canteen to his belt, he bent down, picking up what he thought was a stone. He frowned as he held it up into the light.

'Is this a tooth?'

Amity held out her hand. 'Let me see.'

She turned it over in her fingers. It was long and curved, almost like a tusk. Even in the dim light, Talen could see her face blanch.

'What is it?'

Amity looked back at the paintings. 'The figures, they're all green.'

'What of it?'

Now the rogue trader was running her gloved hand through the patches of fungus that covered parts of the primitive drawings.

'Green figures with big weapons and welding equipment.'

Talen's heart skipped a beat as he realised what she was saying. 'You mean... these are Orks?'

An inhuman roar shook the cargo ship, sending flakes of rust fluttering down from the ceiling like red snow.

CHAPTER SEVEN

String-Guts

'Let go of me!' Zelia yelled, trying to pull her foot from the gretchin's grasp.

The creature giggled, although its amusement turned to a squeal of outrage as Fleapit leant over and flicked a switch on Mekki's wrist-screen, sending the floating engine crashing back down on it.

'No fair!' it wailed, letting go of Zelia's ankle. 'I woz only tryin' to pull meself out, weren't I? Ye said you'd lend an 'and.'

'That doesn't mean you could grab my foot!' Zelia snapped back, jumping up.

The gretchin struggled and twisted,

but was pinned down from the waist by the heavy contraption. There was no way for it to wriggle free.

'I's sorry,' it said, bottom lip quivering. 'Didn't mean to scare ya. I's just a grot. Can't 'arm anyone me, not like da big boyz.'

'You mean Orks,' Mekki said.

The gretchin's eyes brimmed with tears. 'Dey sent me to fetch their whirligig, but it went wrong, didn't it? Smacked down to da ground, with me underneef. Dey'll give me such a beatin' if dey finds me like dis. Dey'll skin me alive.'

Big tears rolled down the gretchin's green face, its tattered ears plastered back against its skull.

'It's da end of String-Guts, dat's fur sure.'

Zelia took a step nearer the snivelling creature.

'Is that your name? String-Guts?'

The gretchin nodded, a big glob of snot hanging from his nose. 'But please, don't tell Badtoof I told ya.'

'Who's that?'

'Badtoof,' String-Guts repeated. 'Badtoof the Rotten. Our leader, 'ee is. Biggest big boy of the Tek-Hedz. 'Ee's gonna mash me into paste.'

The sobs were coming thick and fast now. Zelia could barely understand a word he was saying, although she knew enough about Orks to fill in the gaps. Next to humans, Orks were one of the most widespread races in the galaxy. Gretchin were the smaller of the species, runts of the litter that were press-ganged into service of larger, more savage greenskins. Orks were big on size. The larger and stronger you were, the higher up the food chain you could rise, bullying your way to the top. Bullying smaller gretchin like String-Guts.

'We need to help him,' she concluded, turning to Mekki.

The Martian's eyes widened. 'We cannot. Greenskins are monsters, Zelia Lor. They wreak terror and destruction wherever they bloom.'

'But aren't we no better than them if we leave him here?' She glanced back at the still-snivelling gretchin. She had never seen anyone look so pathetic. 'Look at him. He's not dangerous.'

'You has a good 'eart,' String-Guts told her between sobs. 'We could learn from you, yeah? You better than uzz. You… kind.'

The word sounded so alien to him that it almost broke Zelia's heart.

'String-Guts just wanted to get away,' he continued. 'Away from da big boyz, away from their feet and their fists. Always kickin' String-Guts dey are. Always punchin' 'im. Whack-whack-whack. 'Ad enuff, String-Guts 'as. Don't want it no more. String-Guts wants to be free.'

Zelia turned to Mekki, her mind made up. 'This is what we're going to do. We'll go a safe distance – say, over there by that stream.' She pointed towards the water that burbled behind the trees, an offshoot of the main river. 'Once we're far enough away, we'll activate the grav-packs and he can wriggle free.'

Mekki didn't look convinced. 'I am not sure this is a good idea.'

Fleapit grunted that he thought the same.

'You heard what he said,' Zelia argued. 'The others will beat him if they find him like this. He just wants to get away.'

Mekki looked down at the gretchin, who was gazing up at him imploringly. 'I won't 'urt ya, I promise. Cross me 'eart and 'ope to get sliced into little pieces by a big choppa!'

Mekki sighed. 'Very well, but I do not like it.'

'Oh fank ya, fank ya,' String-Guts preened as they made their way to the brook. 'But 'urry. String-Guts don't feel too clever. I can't move me legz!'

They splashed through the foul-smelling water and stopped on the other side of the brook, looking back at the trapped gretchin. Zelia nodded at Mekki.

'This should be far enough.'

The Martian tapped his screen. 'I hope you are right about this.'

'So do I,' she admitted.

The grav-packs hummed and the contraption rose steadily from the ground, but String-Guts didn't move. He just lay there, beneath the shadow of the hovering machine.

'You can get away now,' Zelia called out, but still he didn't budge.

'Do you think he is all right?' Mekki asked.

Zelia wrung her hands together. 'He said he couldn't move his legs. What if he's paralysed?'

'The grav-packs will not last forever.'

'We can't leave him there.'

Zelia charged through the water and raced towards the still gretchin.

'Zelia Lor,' Mekki called after her. 'What are you doing?'

She didn't answer. Instead she ran up to String-Guts. 'You need to move,' she told him.

The gretchin didn't respond. Zelia nudged him with her foot, but he didn't stir. The poor thing had passed out.

Above them, the grav-packs spluttered.

'They are failing!' Mekki yelled out in warning.

Zelia grabbed the unconscious gretchin and tried to pull him from beneath the floating junk heap. He weighed more than he looked.

'Help me!'

Mekki went to join her, but Fleapit put out a paw to stop him. The Martian hesitated, before running over to help Zelia pull String-Guts clear. He was just in time. The grav-packs cut out and the pile of engine parts and propellers came crashing down.

'We did it!' Zelia cheered, letting go of String-Guts's hands.

'Yeah, ya did,' the gretchin said, suddenly springing up from the floor. Zelia screamed as he grabbed hold of her. She struggled but the gretchin was too strong.

'We tried to help you,' she spluttered.

Instead of answering, String-Guts yelled at the top of his voice, "Elp! 'Elp! I izz being attacked by humies. Humies in the jungle! Humies in the jungle!'

'Let go of her,' Mekki said, launching himself at the gretchin only to be knocked back by a powerful kick.

'Come and save us,' String-Guts shouted. ''Urry!'

There was a commotion in the jungle and two huge figures ploughed out of the trees. These weren't gretchin. At least twice the height of String-Guts, they were as broad as they were tall, muscles bunched under thick green skin. Their wide mouths were crammed full of thick tusks that looked almost as sharp as the metal spikes that jutted out of their shoulder pads.

But scariest of all were the weapons

they held in their massive hands. The brute on the left was wielding the largest, most imposing gun Zelia had ever seen, while his partner – an Ork with a large ring through his nose – held a gigantic armour-plated axe.

'I fawt ya said ya was being attacked?' the Ork with the gun said, glaring at String-Guts.

'I was,' the gretchin lied, 'but I got da uppa hard hand, didn't I? Cuz I'm bigga! Stronga!'

'Yer a little runt,' the axe-wielding Ork said. 'And so are dey. Never seen humies so runty.'

'Dey're young 'uns,' String-Guts said. 'Except for dat hairy one over there.'

'Hairy one?' the gun-toting Ork asked. 'Wot hairy one?'

Zelia twisted in String-Guts's grip, and grinned when she saw that Fleapit had vanished. He was probably hiding in the trees, ready to swoop down and rescue them. Mekki meanwhile had his hands raised in surrender, his eyes fixed on the Ork's gun, which was now pointing straight at him.

'Wot we 'spose to do wiv 'em?' the Axe-Ork asked.

String-Guts sniffed. 'Dunno. Take 'em to Badtoof? 'Ee'll know. 'Ee's smart, ain't he? A right ol' brainbox.'

'Yeah. Take 'em to da boss.' Mekki let out a yelp as the Gun-Ork grabbed him and started trudging away. ''Ee'll know what to do.'

Zelia let the traitorous gretchin drag her after the Orks. There was no point trying to escape, not before Fleapit swung in to rescue them.

She scanned the treetops, looking for a telltale flash of orange fur, but there was no sign of the Jokaero.

He was probably waiting for the right moment.

Any minute now...

CHAPTER EIGHT

Ork Logic

'What is it?' Talen yelled as something large and angry rammed against the cargo ship. The hull buckled and the support beams groaned.

'How am I supposed to know?' Amity snapped, drawing both of her beamers. 'Get behind me and shut off that light.'

Talen reached up and grabbed the spinning lume-compass, the light immediately extinguishing. He stuffed it into his pocket, as another roar and even louder bang heralded more dents appearing in the wall. Talen jumped to his side as hull plates crashed down from the ceiling, only just missing him.

He pulled out his bolas and started spinning the stones on their leather strap.

'I knew I should have brought the Tau suit.'

'The Tau suit you could barely control?'

Talen's cheeks burned at the memory of him desperately trying to control the alien battle armour back on Hinterland. 'Saved your life, didn't I?'

'Shhh!' Amity hissed.

The roaring had stopped, but they could hear a low snuffling like a gigantic pig.

'Stay there,' Amity ordered, stalking towards the open hatch.

'Not likely,' Talen said, creeping after her.

She broke into a run and flattened her back against the hull, beamers held high. 'Then don't blame me if you get your head ripped off.'

'Could I at least have one of those?'

he whispered, nodding towards the pistols.

She considered this. 'No. Now shut up, before you get us both killed.'

He fell silent as they crept towards the open door. The noises outside had stopped, although the entire structure was creaking alarmingly.

Amity paused beside the hatch, before peeking around the door frame.

She was greeted by an immediate bellow. A huge dent appeared behind Talen as whatever was outside launched itself at the ship. He was thrown through the air and he hit the deck hard, throwing up moss and fungi as he rolled. Behind him, Amity unloaded both of her beamers through the open door. A huge scarlet paw burst through the gap, curved talons swiping at her. Amity threw herself to the side, only narrowly avoiding getting disembowelled. The claws tore at the hull, ripping it apart as if the metal hull plates were made of paper. Talen watched in horror

as a gaping hole appeared in the side
of the ship, a huge snout thrusting
in towards them. Mucus snorted from
the massive nostrils, splattering over
Talen, who slipped on the gunk as he
tried to avoid being crushed against the
opposite wall. The red-skinned monster
was the size of a battle tank, with a
wide snapping mouth full of teeth. Its
snarls were deafening in the confined
space, but the noise was nothing
compared to the stink. The creature
reeked of rancid meat. No, Talen
thought to himself, that was unfair.
Rancid meat smelled better!

It thrashed and twisted as it tried to
shove itself into the jagged hole it had
created. It flicked its slab-like head,
swatting Talen from his feet with one
swipe of its gigantic snout. He flew
across the empty hold, landing in a
heap beside Amity who was turning her
laspistols against the paintings on the
wall behind them.

'What are you doing?'

'Trying to blast another way out! Unless you've got a better idea?'

Talen looked back at the snuffling monstrosity. He realised that he had dropped his bolas, and looked around to see the leather straps sticking out from under one of the monster's splayed feet. The thing was standing on them.

Amity cursed as her beamers cut out, their power packs drained. Now they really were trapped.

'Give them to me,' Talen snapped, grabbing at Amity's pistols.

'Why?' she said, snatching them away. 'They're dead!'

'I know. I'm going to throw them at it.'

When Amity didn't hand over the guns, Talen snatched the canteen from his belt and hurled it at the creature. The metal canister smacked into one of its yellow eyes, the wail of pain nearly knocking Talen off his feet. He groped around the floor, trying to find anything else he could use as a projectile. All the time, the monster was trying to drag itself into the hold, its massive jaws snapping together.

Talen lurched forwards, dropping into a roll. His hand shot out, grabbing the straps of his bolas. The monster lunged towards him, raising its foot. Talen pushed himself up into a crouch, his weapon back in his hands. He spun the stones, trying to ignore the mocking voice in the back of his head that wanted to know what he thought he was doing. As if something so small and pathetic could take on something so big. He didn't know if the voice was talking about the bolas, or Talen himself. Still, the canteen had hurt the creature. If they kept fighting back, then maybe it would give up, or at least retreat enough for them to get away.

With a cry of defiance, he released the bolas and the stones whipped forwards, striking a cluster of bloodshot eyes. The monster roared, and – yes! – pulled back slightly.

Talen scuttled forwards, ignoring Amity's warning, to recover the bolas which had bounced from the creature's blubbery hide. That's when he saw the mammoth chains that were wound around the monster's pulsating body.

The thing wasn't retreating; it was being *pulled* out of the wrecked ship, hauled back by muscular handlers.

Amity ran forwards, grabbing Talen and pulling him to his feet. 'You need to look as big as possible.'

'What? Why?'

'Because of them,' the captain said, nodding at the muscled warriors who were holding the creature at bay. They were clad in bone armour, their long, pointed ears sticking out of helmets fashioned from skulls. Their fangs were bared, their arms bulging with the effort of holding back the snarling beast.

'Are those...'

Amity drew her beamers and pointed them at a third greenskin who was

lumbering towards them, a scar over
his left eye.

'Orks,' she confirmed, her fingers
tightening around the triggers.

'But your power packs–'

'Are empty, but they don't know that.
Orks respond to signs of strength. Start
whirling those rocks of yours.'

Talen did as he was told, spinning the
bolas in his hand, but all he wanted
to do was run. The Ork with the scar
over his eye towered over them, a
crossbow loaded with barbed arrows in
his hand. His rough green skin was
smothered in tribal tattoos, his one
good eye as red as blood.

'Oo are you?' the one-eyed Ork
growled.

'Someone you don't want to cross,'
Amity warned him.

'Ha!' the Ork barked. 'I could snap
you like a twig.'

'I'd like to see you try.'

What was she doing? Calling out
an Ork didn't seem like a show of

strength. It seemed a show of stupidity!

One-Eye glanced down at Talen's whirling bolas. Moving faster than Talen would have thought possible, the Ork snatched out a hand, grabbing the spinning stones. He yanked the bolas from Talen's grip, looked at the stones, and clenched his massive fist. The stones ground together as the muscles in the Ork's forearm bunched. When he opened his hand again, sand trickled between his callused fingers, all that remained of Talen's weapon.

The leather straps tumbled to the ground.

Amity didn't flinch, the aim of her useless beamers unwavering. 'What's that thing?' she asked, nodding towards the chained monster.

The Ork glanced at the creature. 'It's a sniffler-squig, ain't it?'

'And what's it supposed to be sniffing out?' Talen asked. 'Us?'

One-Eye laughed. 'Why would we be trackin' pipsqueaks like you?'

'Then what's it looking for?' Amity asked.

The Ork scratched his head. 'I dunno. The warboss knows that stuff.'

'Then how will you know when you've found it?' Talen's question was a genuine one. He'd heard that Orks were stupid, but surely they knew what they were tracking.

'We'll be able to see it, won't we?' the Ork rumbled in reply. 'Wiv our own peepers.'

'But what if you get it wrong?' Amity

asked. 'Won't your boss be angry?'

One-Eye grunted. ''Ee'll be furious.'

'Then shouldn't you ask him?'

'Eh?'

'Shouldn't you ask him what you're looking for, just in case you find it?'

'The humie's got a point,' one of the squig handlers called over.

'Yeah,' agreed the other. 'We don't want Nettle-Nekk blastin' us.'

'That's your warboss?' Talen cut in. 'Nettle-Nekk?'

'He sounds tough,' Amity said.

''Ee is!' One-Eye responded, his voice cracking. Talen couldn't tell if it was from pride or fear. ''Ee's the biggest, baddest warboss there izz.'

'Then you'll want to keep on his good side. Why don't you head back and check what you're supposed to be tracking?'

'Wot about you?' One-Eye asked.

'We'll wait here,' Amity replied, 'you can capture us later. Assuming you do want to capture us.'

'Oh, we wants to catch ya,' One-Eye confirmed. 'Yer humies, ain't ya? We 'ates humies almost as much as we 'ates Tek-Hedz.'

Talen had no idea who Tek-Hedz were but he was happy to let that slide for now. He was too busy thinking that there was no way the Orks would fall for Amity's ploy.

'So you'll wait 'ere?'

Amity nodded. 'We won't move a muscle.'

'While we find out what we're supposed to be trackin'?'

'You've got it.'

'Fair enuff,' One-Eye rumbled, before turning back to the handlers. 'Come on, boyz. Let's go see Nettle-Nekk.'

'Back away, slowly,' Amity whispered as the Ork stomped towards the squig. 'And get ready to run.'

'I can't believe that worked!'

'Ork logic. They may be big...'

'That's an understatement!'

'But their brains are small. We'll be

long gone before they realise they've been duped. *If* they realise.' Her beamers were still aimed at One-Eye's broad back. 'That's it. That's it... now, *run!*'

They turned and sprinted for the trees. They'd almost made it when there was a click from behind, followed by a *thwip!*

Amity cried out as an arrow slammed into her shoulder. She tumbled forwards, a beamer falling from her grasp.

Talen dropped down beside her. 'Are you all right?'

'What do you think?' she snarled through clenched teeth.

He looked up to see One-Eye thudding towards them.

'I've changed me mind,' he growled. 'Yer coming with us, just in case we forget what we're supposed to ask Nettle-Nekk.' His crossbow swung up to aim at Talen. Another bolt had already clicked into place and was ready to fire.

'Unless you've got somewhere to go?'

Talen raised his hands and shook his head.

There was nowhere to run.

CHAPTER NINE

Badtoof

'Talen. Come in please. Talen.'

'What you doing back dere?'

Zelia let her sleeve drop, hiding the vox from String-Guts.

'Nothing. Just talking to myself.'

'Stupid humies,' the gretchin concluded, scampering back to walk with the Orks, who were dragging Mekki and Zelia along in a net.

Zelia wanted to cry. She wanted to scream and shout and kick at the thick ropes that enveloped them. Since being captured by the Orks they'd been dragged through thorn-weeds and thudded over logs. They were smothered in mud, the disgusting muck stinging the countless scratches and grazes they'd suffered as the Orks tramped through the undergrowth.

Worst of all were the rivers. Zelia and Mekki had tried to keep their mouths shut as the Orks had swum from bank to bank, afraid of what diseases might lurk in the putrid water, not to mention the tentacled eels that writhed beneath the surface. It was no good, though. The shock of being plunged into icy water had proved too much. Zelia and Mekki had flailed around the net, unable to see, the water little more than a brown sludge. They gasped and spluttered as they were dragged up the other side, coughing up syrupy water from burning lungs.

And that was before they spotted the swollen horn-leeches crawling over their clothes to get to their skin.

How the Orks had laughed as Zelia and Mekki squirmed, swiping the slimy creatures from their bruised arms and legs.

'Dunk 'em again,' String-Guts had squealed happily. 'Dunk 'em again.'

Zelia had forced herself not to complain, trying to remain strong. Beside her, Mekki clung onto the net, muttering calculations beneath his breath to keep calm.

If only she could do the same... or could stop reminding herself that this was all her fault. She had been the one who insisted they came to this Ork-infested planet in the first place. But she could only hang on, as the Orks dropped beneath giant logs to hide from a lumbering ape with long pointed quills for fur. She didn't know what it was; all Zelia knew was that if Orks didn't want to mess with the thing, two frightened children wouldn't stand a chance.

When they finally arrived at their destination, the Orks' camp was as bad as she'd imagined. The greenskins had chopped down a swathe of trees, using the stumps as worktables for ramshackle machines that belched nauseating smoke into the air. Even if Zelia had got through to Talen, she wouldn't have been able to hear what he was saying above the roar of the mismatched technology. Then there were the brutish shouts of the Orks themselves, hundreds of them clanging tools and openly brawling between metal shacks that looked like they had been constructed by a child with a welding gun and very little understanding of architecture.

No one took any notice of them as they were dragged through the mud. The greenskins were too busy working, or fighting, sometimes both at the same time.

There were Orks rounding up little blob-shaped critters, Orks hammering weapons in and out of shape and Orks extracting their own tusks with rusty pliers. Zelia stared as a greenskin plucked out one of its teeth, only to exchange the fang for a bowl of slop. Is that what Orks used as money? Their own teeth?

Their captors lugged them towards a large crowd who were watching two enormous Orks knocking lumps out of each other. Each punch shook the ground and was accompanied by whoops and cheers from the crowd. It was difficult to make out the two combatants. The larger of the two wore riveted armour, the bottom of his face covered in an iron jaw complete with jagged teeth. He wore a chunky metal gauntlet over his right hand, while a hairy creature was perched on his bald head like a wriggling wig.

His opponent wore leather armour studded with large spikes. He was a head smaller than his bewigged rival, but had the upper hand, steel knuckledusters clanging off the larger Ork's jaw-guard.

Zelia winced every time the

leather-clad combatant landed a punch, and the mob went wild as the larger of the two staggered back. The blows were coming thick and fast now, the smaller Ork finding his rhythm. For all his armour, the larger fighter couldn't respond, his head snapping back and forth with every strike.

And then, out of nowhere, the larger combatant swung up his gauntleted fist. A punishing uppercut connected with the smaller Ork's jaw. He staggered back, his red eyes rolling in their deep sockets. He swung a punch, but missed, only to receive another blow to the head. He tottered for a moment, punch-drunk, and then toppled over, hitting the ground hard. Even then, the larger Ork didn't break off his attack. He grabbed the smaller greenskin's feet and swung the Ork back and forth, slamming him into the dirt, left and right and left and right. The leather-clad Ork could only flail helplessly as he was pummelled repeatedly into the ground.

The crowd cheered as the larger Ork whirled his defeated challenger around and around by the ankles, letting go to send him soaring through the air. The leather-clad Ork slammed into a tree, ricocheting off the tough bark to crash down onto a nearby gunship, its thick metal roof buckling beneath the sudden weight.

The crowd roared, driven wild with bloodlust, and fired their oversized shootas into the air. Empty shells rained down as the victor stood, breathing heavily, never taking his eyes from his fallen foe.

As they watched, a gaggle of greenskins clambered on top of the gunship and dragged the dazed Ork away.

The victor turned and threw his muscled arms into the air.

'Oo'z da biggest and da baddest?' he roared, the crowd responding as one.

'You are, boss!'

'Oo can't be beat?'

'You can't, boss!'

'Oo will rip off yer arms and use them to smack you around da head if ya even look at 'im funny?'

'You will, boss!'

The armour-clad Ork punched the air as his tribe chanted his name over and over.

'Badtoof! Badtoof! Badtoof! Badtoof!'

The warboss grinned, his eyes falling on Zelia and Mekki still trussed up in their sack.

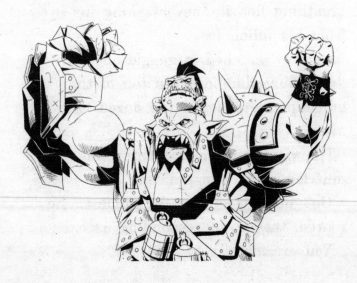

'Quiet!' he bellowed, and the mob fell silent. Badtoof stomped towards them, and Zelia scuttled back, worried for a second that he was going to grind them into the mud with a booted foot. 'Oi, oi. Wot's all dis?'

'I found 'em,' String-Guts piped up, cringing in front of his warboss. 'In the jungle.'

'And wot was dey doing in the jungle?' Badtoof the Rotten asked, his lips drawing back to reveal stained tusks that more than lived up to his name.

'Just walkin', boss,' the gretchin replied.

'Just walkin'? Just walkin'? No one walks in da jungle unless I allows it. No one does nuffink without me say-so.'

'We're sorry,' Zelia stammered, throwing up a hand to block the spit that sprayed from Badtoof's wide lips. 'We were just trying to get to our ship.'

Badtoof's eyes lit up at the mention of the *Profiteer.* 'A good ship, izz it?'

Zelia nodded. 'Yeah. The best.'

The warboss raised his hands to the sky. 'Then it's *my* ship!'

'What?' she stammered. 'No!'

'Where izz it?'

String-Guts poked at Zelia through the net. 'Tell 'im. Tell 'im where 'ee can find 'is ship.'

'But it is not his ship,' Mekki insisted. 'It belongs to Captain Amity. You must let us go.'

Badtoof threw back his head and laughed. 'Oh I must, must I? Ha ha ha! I like dese runts. Dey're funny.' He turned to the gretchin. 'You did well, Worm-Guts.'

'String-Guts, boss.'

'Wot?'

'Me name... it's String-Guts.'

'If I says yer name is Worm-Guts, it's Worm-Guts, understand?' the warboss bellowed, making his point by booting the gretchin over the heads of the crowd. The Orks cheered in unison as he landed in a heap on the other side of the camp.

'Yes, boss,' String-Guts shouted from the ground, unwilling or maybe unable to get back up. 'Worm-Guts it is.'

'Better,' Badtoof said, turning his attention back to Zelia and Mekki. 'Now, ya gonna tell me where to find dis ship, or not?'

The thunder of approaching engines distracted the warboss before he could punctuate his question with his fists. The crowd parted as three Orks roared into the camp on the back of low-slung warbikes. The riders wore helmets and goggles, and held vicious-looking weapons in their hands: chains, maces and, in the case of the leader, a length of pipe studded with long rusty nails.

The bikes screeched to a halt in front of Badtoof, smothering the crowd in choking fumes.

''Ere dey are,' Badtoof bellowed in greeting, seemingly forgetting about Zelia and Mekki. 'Me bike-boyz, back where dey belong.'

The leader of the mob leapt from his

bike, and immediately swung his fist at the warboss. Badtoof blocked the blow and thumped the biker in the face, knocking out a large tooth. The tusk landed by Zelia and Mekki's sack as the two Orks headbutted each other in greeting.

The crowd cheered as the two Orks began to wrestle, but Zelia didn't mind as long as it kept Badtoof busy.

Reaching through the net, she grabbed the biker's dislodged tooth. She tested the edge of the fang against her thumb. It was sharp, but would it be sharp enough?

While Badtoof and the biker tussled, Zelia went to work, sawing through the thick rope with the jagged fang.

CHAPTER TEN

Nettle-Nekk

On the other side of the jungle, Talen and Amity were dragged in front of another, equally terrifying warboss.

Talen tried to keep his head up as they were pushed forwards. He was scared – boy, was he scared – but he didn't want to show it, not with so many greenskins watching their every move.

'I suppose you're Nettle-Nekk,' he said, trying to disguise the fear in his voice.

'Oo else would I be, eh?' the warboss sneered from his throne of skulls. 'Yer in da lair of the Snake-Skull Clan, ain't ya? Course I'm Nettle-Nekk.'

Like the rest of his tribe, the warboss was smothered in tattoos, although he didn't cover his inked skin with armour. He wore only leather breeches and heavy boots, and most of his scarred chest was hidden behind a bushy and obviously fake beard. The beard wasn't made of hair, or even fur, but what looked like fang-nettles woven into a thick mat.

The warboss scratched at the beard as he ordered for Talen and Amity to

be shoved forwards, wincing slightly as the barbed stalks stung his already blistered fingers.

But Talen didn't care about Nettle-Nekk's throbbing fingertips. All that mattered to him was Amity, who still had One-Eye's arrow sticking out of her shoulder. The rogue trader swayed on her feet, her skin waxy and eyes red-rimmed. Every move must have been agony, and yet she was trying her hardest to stand straight.

'Remember,' she had hissed as they had been led into the clan's lair. 'Show no weakness.'

That was easier said than done.

'Da question is...' Nettle-Nekk said, pointing a slab-like finger at Talen and Amity, 'wot are you?'

'Dey are humies, boss,' One-Eye replied, proudly standing beside the sniffler-squig still straining at its chains.

'I can see dey is humies. I just wanna know why I's lookin' at their scrawny faces when I should be lookin' at da Biggun.'

One-Eye opened his mouth to speak, but hesitated. 'I-I can't remember, boss. There was sumfink about a question I had to ask you.'

Nettle-Nekk roared in frustration, pulling a skull from his throne and chucking it at One-Eye.

'I knew it woz a mistake to send ya, ya worthless guffbag. What did I say?'

'You said it woz a mistake, boss.'

'But I don't make mistakes, do I?'

One-Eye shook his head. 'No, boss. You don't, boss.'

'So what izz I 'spose to do with humies?'

'Dey are clever, boss,' One-Eye stammered. 'Dey got brains in their bonces. Dey could 'elp.'

''Elp wiv wot?'

One-Eye swallowed. 'Wiv whatever it was I've forgotten.'

Nettle-Nekk snarled, rubbing his fake beard into his own face.

'Doesn't that hurt?' Talen heard someone ask. It took him a moment to realise that the voice was his own.

'Wot?' Nettle-Nekk rumbled.

Talen tried not to tremble as he repeated the question he hadn't meant to ask out loud. 'Your beard... doesn't it hurt you?'

'Of course it 'urts,' the warboss snapped. 'Wot's the point of nettles if dey don't 'urt. Keep me on me toes, don't it?' He tapped his flat head. 'Keeps me brain-box buzzing. We needz to be ready.'

'Ready for what?' Amity croaked.

'For the Tek-Hedz to strike, wot else?'

'And they're your enemy?' Talen asked. 'A rival clan?' If there was one thing he understood, it was gang warfare.

'Dey are scumbags, dat's what they is,' Nettle-Nekk bellowed. 'Dey carve up the jungle with their filthy, stinkin' engines. Dey don't give a fig about the green stuff.'

'The green stuff? You mean... nature.'

'Told ya dey had brains, boss,'
One-Eye said.

'Shut yer gob or I'll turn ya inside out,' Nettle-Nekk barked. 'Got it?'

'Got it,' One-Eye confirmed.

The warboss glared at Talen. 'Course I meanz nature. Look around ya. We loves nature. We protect nature, to the deff!'

'To the deff!' his Orks echoed as one.

'And that's why you don't use machines?' Talen asked.

He'd noticed the lack of engines the moment they'd been hauled into the camp. He'd been brought up on horror stories about Orks, his father desperate to frighten him into fighting the Emperor's wars. According to Tyrian Stormweaver, Orks loved machines, the bigger and noisier the better. They rode into battle on crudely constructed war machines that were little more than deathtraps. That suited the Orks. They didn't mind getting blown up, as long as they took out the enemy in the process.

It explained the wrecks back at the ship graveyard, but here there were hardly any machines, and those the greenskins toiled over were made of wood or stone. These Ork carpenters banged nails into planks with their fists, or carved battering rams out of twisted tree trunks. Others stirred cauldrons of foul-smelling gunk. Surely that wasn't what they ate? No, Talen saw gretchin pouring the gloop into wooden grenades. They were some kind of bombs.

There were no signs of guns or cannons either. Nettle-Nekk's Orks were armed with bows and spears, all of which looked as if they could cause serious damage.

'The Tek-Hedz use machines. Dey use metal and oil and all that gubbinz. Not us. We use wood and stone and wood.'

'Err... you already said wood, boss,' One-Eye pointed out.

Another skull flew at the Ork. At this rate, Nettle-Nekk wouldn't have much of his throne left.

'But none of dat explains why you izz 'ere!' the warlord said, turning his attention back to the prisoners.

'Answer da boss!' One-Eye said, grabbing Amity, who tried to stifle a cry of pain.

'Wot's wrong wiv 'im?' Nettle-Nekk asked, peering at the rogue trader.

'*She's* hurt,' Talen told the boss.

'I stuck 'im,' One-Eye said proudly.

'*Her!*' Talen corrected.

The ork shrugged. 'Wotever.'

'Talen, don't...' Amity hissed. 'If they think I'm weak...'

'You need her,' Talen said quickly.

Nettle-Nekk looked baffled by the comment. 'I does?'

'She's the best captain in the galaxy. She knows loads about... about battles and stuff.'

'*I* know about battles,' the warboss barked jumping up from his throne, saliva dripping from his fangs. 'I've been fightin' battles all me life!'

He took a step forwards, looming over

Talen, so big he blotted out the sun.

'Dere ain't nuffink a stoopid humie could teach me about *Waaagh!* Nuffink!'

'Okay,' Talen squeaked, trying to think on his feet. 'But maybe she can help me.'

"Elp you? Do wot? Escape?' His hands had curled into fists the size of boulders. 'Do you fink you can escape da Snake-Skulls?'

'No,' Talen stammered, 'I find things. I'm a tracker.'

'I already 'as a tracker,' Nettle-Nekk said, pointing at the sniffler.

'Yeah, but not like me. I can find anything you want... like the Biggun.'

Nettle-Nekk snorted. 'You don't even know what da Biggun izz, stupid little runt!'

'Then tell me, and I'll find it for you.'

'Wot do you fink it is? It's a squig, ain't it? A coloss... a calloss... a ded big squig.'

'Like that thing?' Talen said, glancing at the sniffler.

'Bigger dan dat,' Nettle-Nekk said.

'Biggest there's ever been.'

'And why do you want it?'

'To beat da Tek-Hedz, wot else?'

At the mention of their enemy's defeat the Snake-Skulls roared, One-Eye chanting *'Waaagh! Waaagh!'* over and over again.

Nettle-Nekk added to the racket by slamming a giant fist against his equally humongous chest.

'We've been fighting dis *Waaagh!* for years, ain't we?' he bellowed. 'Dey 'ave their shootas, we 'ave our arras.'

'Arras?'

Nettle-Nekk jabbed at the bolt sticking out of Amity's shoulder. 'Arras! Darts! We 'its dem, dey 'its us. On and on it goes. Year after year.'

'You've reached an impasse,' Amity said, looking paler than ever.

Nettle-Nekk hauled Amity up to face him, the sudden movement causing her to cry out all over again.

'Wot's dat supposed to mean?' the warboss snarled, looking like he was about to twist her head off to see if the answer was inside.

'A stalemate,' she shouted back, suppressing a sob. 'Deadlock. Both sides evenly matched.'

Nettle-Nekk threw Amity to the ground, and this time she screamed with the pain. Talen dropped down beside her.

'Leave her alone!' he yelled, but Nettle-Nekk wasn't listening.

'We're betta dan da Tek-Hedz!' he roared. 'Stronga.'

'And yet you can't beat them,' Amity hissed.

'Course we can beat 'em!' Nettle-Nekk thundered, raising his fists. 'We'll beat 'em good, once we beat you!'

'We can help you find the Biggun!' Amity yelled. 'We know how to find it!'

That stopped Nettle-Nekk in his tracks. He froze, before bellowing at his chanting mob.

'Shaddup! Let me listen to da humie. Qui-aaaat!'

The crowd fell silent and Nettle-Nekk turned back to them.

"Ow? 'Ow ya gonna find da Biggun?"

Amity looked like she was going to pass out, so Talen jumped in.

'That's the trick. We don't have to find the Biggun. I'll make it come to us.'

'Naaargh!' Nettle-Nekk growled. 'Yer wastin' me time. No one can make da Biggun do nuffink.'

Talen raised his hands, as if they would stop Nettle-Nekk pummelling him into the ground. 'Yes, you can. Back home, I used to catch sewer rats for my gang.'

'De Biggun ain't no rat.'

'No, but we can trap it the same way... using bait. We used to put out scraps of bread soaked in fat. It worked every time. The rats came running and...' Talen slapped his hands together. 'Snap!'

'Snap?'

'We sprang our trap.'

'Snap!' Nettle-Nekk boomed. 'I likes

that. Snap, snap, snap!'

Talen grinned as the entire warband started making snapping noises. He had them now.

'So what do you think?'

Nettle-Nekk's lips pulled back into a horrible leer. 'I fink we're gonna win da *Waaagh!*'

CHAPTER ELEVEN

A Feast Fit
for a Warboss

'What d'ya mean ya didn't find 'er?'
Badtoof hollered at the bikers. Zelia
hadn't really been listening to the
conversation. With Mekki shielding
what she was doing, she had been too
busy sawing through the ropes with the
tooth. Piecing together what little she'd
heard, the bikers had been sent out
to find something the Orks called the
Biggun, a gigantic monster the Tek-Hedz
needed to beat their arch-enemies, the
Snake-Skulls. Apparently, the rival clan
also had the same idea, and Badtoof

wanted to make sure that the Tek-Hedz found it first. By the sound of it, both tribes had been searching for the mythical beast for ages.

'I'm sorry, boss,' one of the bikers said. 'We looked real 'ard.'

'Not 'ard enuff,' Badtoof yelled, smacking the lead biker with his gauntlet. 'Take 'em away. I don't wanna see their stupid faces no more.'

The bikers were mobbed by Badtoof's followers and dragged away.

Zelia carried on working as Badtoof stomped around yelling his head off. She'd almost sliced through the rope. It would make a hole in the net big enough for them to wriggle through.

'You okay, boss?' one of the sniffler handlers asked.

'Am I okay? AM I OKAY?' the warboss parroted. 'Of course I ain't okay. Punch yerself in the face.'

'Wot?'

'You got problems with yer lugholes?'

'No, boss. Sorry, boss.' There was a

thwack as the Ork thumped itself.

"Arder!'

'Yes, boss.'

Thwack!

'Again!'

THWACK!

The rope twanged as Zelia cut
through the last few threads.

'It's no good,' Badtoof said. 'I'm too
angry to enjoy mindless violence. Wot's
da world coming to, eh?'

Someone scuttled through the crowd.
It was String-Guts. 'You know wot'll
make you feel betta, boss?'

'No, wot?'

'Grub! You loves a slap-up meal.'

Badtoof considered this, and nodded.
'Yer right, Worm-Guts, I do. Where's da
Grub-Grot?'

Another gretchin ran up. It was fatter
than String-Guts and wore a wonky
chef's hat on its pointed head and a
stained apron around its plump belly.
It held not one but two massive meat
cleavers.

'Ye want sumfink to eat, boss?'

'Yeah, I'm starving! Wot you got?'

The Grub-Grot started to reel off the delicacies on offer, most of which seemed to involve something called a squig, which Zelia could only assume were the blobby little creatures she'd seen earlier. There was roast squig, boiled squig, raw squig, chopped squig, squig pie, squig stew, squig hash and squig salad.

'Wot's squig salad?' the warboss asked.

'It's a squig with a lettuce stuck in its gob!'

'Yuck! Sounds 'orrible. I'm fed up with squig. All we eats izz squig. I want sumfink new. I wants sumfink *different*.'

This was their chance. Zelia squeezed through the hole in the net, pulling it wide so Mekki could crawl out. All around the Tek-Hedz were yelling out things their warboss could eat, from shootas to rocks. Zelia grabbed Mekki's hand and ran, hoping to get away while the greenskins were otherwise occupied.

Glancing over her shoulder, she slammed straight into String-Guts.

'Where d'ya fink yer going'?' the gretchin asked.

'Er, to find something for Badtoof to eat,' she said, thinking on her feet.

'No need,' String-Guts said, grabbing them. 'I've got just da thing.' He dragged them back towards Badtoof. 'Oi, boss. What about roasted humie?'

Badtoof licked his lips with a thick, slug-like tongue.

'Now yer talkin'! Sounds deeelicious!'

'We need to get out of here!' Zelia snapped at Mekki as she struggled against the ropes.

'The thought had occurred to me,' Mekki replied, trying his hardest to reach the coarse knots.

They were tied back to back on a spit that was slowly being turned by the Grub-Grot, while Badtoof slobbered in anticipation, a knife and fork already in hand.

The rest of the clan were gathered around the open fire, cheering, shouting and – rather predictably – fighting each other. String-Guts meanwhile was sitting at his warboss's feet, a jug of grog in his scrawny hands.

'What are we going to do?' Zelia asked.

'Give them indigestion?' Mekki suggested, turning his head from the flames. The heat was intense. Zelia choked, barely able to see through the smoke as the spit turned to face Badtoof.

'We won't fill you up, you know,' she shouted at the warboss, tears streaming down her soot-covered face. 'There's hardly any meat on me, and Mekki's as skinny as a rake.'

'Zelia Lor is correct,' the Martian agreed, trying to hide the desperation in his voice. 'We will hardly make a satisfying meal.'

'Meal?' the warboss sniggered. 'Yer not a meal. Yer a *snack*, for the evening's entertainment.'

'Entertainment?' Mekki repeated, seizing on the word. 'If it is entertainment that you require, I would be happy to oblige.'

Zelia heard an 'oooooh' erupt from the crowd, and craned her neck to see that Mekki was projecting a hololith into the air. It was the holo of the Space Marine that he had used to trick the Necron Hunter back on the ice planet. Badtoof jumped to his feet, clenching his crude cutlery with such force that the fork buckled in his fist.

'Wot's dis?' he demanded. 'Magik?'

'Yes,' Mekki called back. 'Magic. I can use my magic to tell you stories that would make your tusks curl.'

The Space Marine was replaced with an image of Targian exploding, then of Necron scythe-ships atomising space cruisers.

'I likes it,' Badtoof cooed, red eyes full of wonder. 'I likes it a lot. Show me more! More!'

Mekki scrolled through his

memory-wafers, the images revolving in time with the spit.

The Necron Hunter.  Genestealers chasing through corridors of a wrecked ship.

A Tau battlesuit firing wildly, out of control.

Badtoof clashed his cutlery together. 'Dis is brilliant. Absolutely zoggin' brilliant. Wot else can ya do?'

'He can invent things!' Zelia shouted out. 'Amazing things.'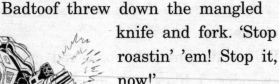

'Wot fings?'

'Anything you want. Skimmers? Warbuggies? Maybe even a spaceship of your own?'

Badtoof threw down the mangled knife and fork. 'Stop roastin' 'em! Stop it, now!'

Beside him, String-Guts looked

crestfallen. 'You sure, boss?'

'Dey're too good to eat,' the warboss announced, pointing at the Grub-Grot. 'Step away from dat turny-thingy before I twist yer fat 'ead from yer shoulders.'

The chef did as he was told, although the flames continued to rage.

'Er. Still a bit hot over here,' Zelia pointed out.

Badtoof blew out the fire as if it were candles on a birthday cake.

'Thanks,' she said, sweat dripping from her brow. 'You won't regret it.'

'I knows I won't. Cut 'em down, ladz. Dey're gonna join in da fun.'

'Join in?' Mekki asked as rough hands ripped the ropes from their wrists. 'What does that mean?'

'Perhaps he's going to invite us to watch the entertainment?' Zelia asked, but she was wrong.

Very, very wrong.

Half an hour later, Zelia and Mekki were standing in a cage, dressed head to sweaty toe in ridiculously heavy armour.

'This isn't what I had in mind,' Zelia whimpered as she watched Badtoof through the bars. The warboss was sitting on a raised platform, surrounded by his followers, who were cheering, belching and singing what could loosely be described as songs... but only if you had never actually heard music before.

String-Guts grunted as he shoved a length of pipe into her hands. She dropped it immediately. It was far too heavy.

'Pick dat up!' the gretchin snapped at her.

'I can't,' she told him. It wasn't a lie. She could barely move her arm.

'Then you better hope yer mate can't hold 'is mace,' String-Guts said, pushing a spiked weapon into Mekki's armoured palm.

'I don't understand,' she admitted.

'And there I was finkin' ya was bright. Ya said yer mate was clever. That 'ee could invent stuff.'

'I can,' Mekki said, his voice muffled by the helmet that had been slapped over his head.

'Then the boss wants to see 'ow inventive ya izz when it comes to pulverising yer enemies.'

'But I have no enemies,' Mekki insisted.

'In da ring, ya do!' String-Guts said, jabbing a finger in Zelia's direction. ''Er!'

She swallowed. 'What? You can't mean...'

'I am afraid he does,' Mekki said, as String-Guts giggled. 'Badtoof was not inviting us to watch the evening's entertainment...'

'We *are* the evening's entertainment,' she groaned.

String-Guts clapped his hands together.

'Dis is gonna be so much fun. A fight to the deff. I always luv a fight to the deff!'

CHAPTER TWELVE

Bait

In the middle of the jungle, Talen
wished he had never mentioned the
word 'bait'.

At first, he'd thought everything would
be all right. Nettle-Nekk had reacted
well to Talen's suggestion. The warboss
had even pulled the arrow from Amity's
shoulder himself and ordered one of
his Painboyz – a lumbering Ork medic
with a hook for a hand – to treat the
wound. This mainly involved slathering
Amity's shoulder in a foul-smelling
ointment which took her mind off the
pain by making her gag.

But the slathering hadn't stopped there. Talen and Amity had been daubed in bright colours, applied liberally by a pack of gretchin. Talen had assumed that they were war paints, that he and the rogue trader were being accepted into Nettle-Nekk's tribe. Then came the shells and stones that were attached to their clothes with sharp wooden pins. They rattled and clanked at the merest movement, which Talen pointed out wasn't great when hunting. He needed to be stealthy. Silent.

Nettle-Nekk grinned. 'Nah ya don't, humie. We want ya making as much noise as possible.'

It soon became clear why. Talen and Amity were grabbed and bundled onto a chariot pulled by a horse-sized squig. The chariot had spikes sticking out of its huge wooden wheels and drums bolted to its sides.

Jumping onto an even larger carriage pulled by four squigs, Nettle-Nekk led the way as they thundered into the jungle. Talen counted five more chariots behind them, overloaded with Orks carrying all manners of spears, bows and clubs. There were nets, ropes and snares, and – strangest of all – a large pole. It was fashioned like a stake, with one end sharpened into a point. Were they planning to throw it at the Biggun like a harpoon?

After they'd been jolted and jostled by the bumpy ride, Nettle-Nekk ordered for them to stop. The convoy skidded to a halt, the squigs foaming at the mouth. Amity had spent the entire time hanging onto the side of the chariot, her face pale.

Talen was about to ask her how her shoulder was doing, when they were pushed from the back of the vehicle.

Talen had bitten his tongue. He'd wanted to fight back, but knew he had to keep the Orks onside. Instead, he'd asked Nettle-Nekk what they were going to use as a lure for the colossal squig.

Now he knew.

The giant stake had been hammered into the ground and the Orks had grabbed Talen and Amity, tying their wrists together with long lengths of rope. Then the ropes were tied to the wooden post.

They were the bait.

Sniggering, the Orks melted into the jungle, hiding behind leaves and trees. Talen could feel their double-crossing gaze on his paint-daubed skin.

Watching.

Waiting.

Talen strained against his rope but it was too thick. There was no way he'd be able to break it. To make things worse, every movement just made the shells rattle.

Not that they had to worry about keeping quiet. Nettle-Nekk had obviously got bored waiting in the shadows and ordered his minions to speed up proceedings. The sound of drums being bashed thundered from the trees.

Boom. Boom. Boom. Boom.

'Now what are they doing?' Talen
asked.

'Trying to attract the Biggun's
attention?' Amity suggested.

She slumped to the ground, the shells
cracking beneath her.

'Are you okay?' Talen said, dropping to
his knee.

'Make out I've fainted. Even call for
help. I doubt the greenskins will care.'

'Why?'

'Just do it.'

Talen shrugged and shouted into the
trees, struggling to be heard over the
beating drums. 'We need your help!
She's lost too much blood!'

As Amity predicted, no Orks came
running.

'Please! I think she's dying.'

'Not bad,' Amity smirked, keeping her
head down low. 'You're wasted as a
ganger. You should be on the stage.'

She lifted her arm slightly so he
could see a big dollop of oily paint on
her sleeve.

'Rub that over the ropes around your wrists.'

Talen looked at the paint and then grinned, realising what the captain had in mind.

He did what she said, coating the ropes with the stuff. It felt disgusting against his skin and smelled even worse, but had an immediate effect.

'Can you slip your hand through the loop?' Amity whispered.

Talen tried, and felt his wrist shift between the slick ropes. He bunched up his fingers, making his hand as small as possible, and pulled with all his might. Inch by inch, his hand slipped through the wet hoop until it popped free with a squelch.

Taking care to hide his movements, Talen smeared as much paint as he could over his other wrist and yanked it out of the knot.

'Shall I do the same for you?'

Amity was still pretending to be

unconscious. 'No need. See my skull brooch?'

'Yeah?'

'Unpin it.'

He knew enough about Amity's jewellery not to ask questions. Since he'd met the rogue trader, the various buttons on her coat had so far summoned her servitor and acted as a flash grenade, not to mention controlling the spinning lume-compass in the cargo ship. He wondered what other gadgets were hidden away in the rest of her jewellery.

'Can we call for Grunt?' he asked as he removed the bronze brooch.

'The homing beacon only operates on a low-frequency vox-channel,' she said. 'He'll be out of range.'

'Then what am I supposed to do with this?' he said, holding the brooch in his hand.

'Aim the end of the pin at the rope around my wrists.'

He did as he was instructed. 'Like this?'

'That's it. Now do you see the skull? Press the metal between the eye sockets.'

'Like this?'

Talen felt a click beneath his thumb and a thin beam of light shot from the end of the pin and burned into the rope that bound Amity's wrists.

'Careful,' she said as a wisp of smoke rose between her hands. 'I'd rather you didn't slice through my skin by mistake.'

'It's a laser?'

'A micro-laser, yes, and it hasn't much charge, so hold it steady.'

She manoeuvred her hands so the laser beam cut through the fraying ropes. Then the thin beam spluttered and died.

'You weren't joking about the charge,'

he said, clicking the skull to no avail.

'It lasted long enough,' Amity said, pulling her hands free and taking back the brooch.

'So we're free,' Talen said as she reattached it to her coat.

'But how do we escape when we're being watched by at least a dozen Orks?'

'You read my mind.'

'Simple... we run!'

'What? Wait!'

Amity leapt to her feet and pelted towards the trees. Talen scrabbled after her, ducking as Snake-Skull arrows flew from the shadows. Talen and Amity threw themselves forwards, the arrows thudding into tree trunks to quiver and vibrate. Talen rolled, disappearing into the undergrowth.

'How did you know we wouldn't run into one of Nettle-Nekk's Orks?' Talen asked.

'I didn't,' Amity said, swallowing. The sudden movement had obviously put a strain on her injured shoulder. 'First rule of rogue trading – sometimes you have to rely on luck.'

'What's the second rule?'

'Don't get caught.'

With a crash, Nettle-Nekk's warband broke cover and ran to the now empty post, oversized weapons brandished and teeth bared.

'Where is dey?' the warboss screamed. 'Don't let 'em get away.'

Talen shifted, and froze as the shells clanked. He held his breath, but the Orks hadn't heard. They were too busy sweeping their weapons through the undergrowth like scythes. Still, there was no way they could escape with all these things bashing together. Then he smiled.

Amity looked puzzled as Talen pulled

a handful of the shells from his jacket and hurled them towards a nearby tree. They clacked against the fungus-strewn tree trunk and clattered to the ground. As one, the Ork horde turned towards the noise and let loose another volley of arrows.

Amity grinned. 'I like the way you think, kid.'

She joined in, throwing shells and stones with her good arm. The Orks whirled around with every smack and tinkle, firing in every direction but the right one. Talen and Amity ran deeper into the trees, lobbing noisy shells as they fled.

One of the Orks' chariots was nearby, its squig merrily munching on fern leaves while a gretchin made repairs to one of the wheels.

Talen and Amity raced for it, only to be stopped in their tracks by an Orkish yell. It was One-Eye, hefting a bazooka over his shoulder. The weapon had been constructed from a hollowed-out log.

'I've found 'em!' he shouted, squeezing the trigger. Talen pulled Amity to the ground as a giant nut burst from the bazooka and impacted against a tree. Talen threw up his arms, expecting a fireball, but instead of exploding into flames the nut erupted into a mass of writhing vines. They wrapped around the tree trunk, encasing the bark in an intricate lattice of thin creepers.

'A bind-weed bomb!' Amity exclaimed. 'Now I've seen it all.'

'Wanna closer look?' One-Eye snarled, charging at them, his bazooka raised like a club.

Talen scraped a dollop of yellow gloop from his leg and flung it up at the stampeding Ork. It splatted against the greenskin's good eye.

'Aaargh! I can't see!' One-Eye screamed, pawing at his face. He tripped on a root and smacked down, the bazooka rolling towards Talen. The ganger snatched it up and ran towards the chariot, firing another nut at the gretchin. The missile exploded, the sudden burst of bind-weed tying him to the spokes of the wheel.

'I like this thing,' said Talen, leaping onto the back of the chariot.

'How much ammo do you have?' Amity said, taking the reins.

He shook the log, listening to the nuts rattle. 'I don't know. Maybe enough for four shots.'

Behind them One-Eye was back on his feet and charging straight for them, his face streaked with the yellow paint. Talen took aim and hit him square in the chest with another bind-weed bomb. The Ork went down, the vines tying his arms to his sides.

'Actually, make that three,' Talen said. 'Drive.'

Amity cracked the reins and the squig roared. It shot forwards, the ensnared gretchin squealing as it spun around and around on the wheel.

Talen squeezed off another shot as they plunged deep into the jungle.

CHAPTER THIRTEEN

Fight! Fight! Fight!

In the Tek-Hedz camp, Badtoof was
laughing his head off. His warbikers
were in the middle of the arena being
forced to take part in a face-biter
competition. From what Zelia could
make out, the rules of the 'game'
basically involved trying to eat a
particularly nasty squig before it ate
you. It was absolutely barbaric, but
the crowd was loving every twisted
minute. They cheered and fired their
weapons into the air. The artillery
fire would have been unbearable if it
wasn't being drowned out by an Ork

thrashing out the greenskin equivalent of a song on an instrument that was half electro-guitar and half anti-aircraft weapon.

Squigs were everywhere, and not just the face-biting variety. They were being eaten between stale buns, thrown at the contestants to put them off and even used to lubricate machines, Mek-Orks squirting an oil-like substance from the trunks of the fat-bellied squiggly beasts.

And Badtoof was still wearing his

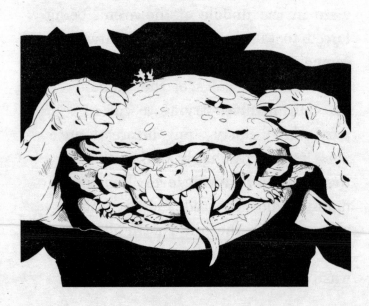

wig-squig, although the poor creature didn't seem to like the noise and spent most of the competition trying to squirm from the warboss's head. In the end, Badtoof clamped it in place with a large horned helmet.

Zelia didn't have time to feel sorry for the living hairpiece. She had her own worries. Only one of the bikers was still standing, which meant it was nearly time for Zelia and Mekki to fight. When the pipe had proved to be too heavy for her, she was handed a giant sword. It was even worse. She tried to use it to chop their way out of the cage, but could hardly lift the blade. What was she supposed to do in the ring if she couldn't wield her weapon? Obviously, she didn't want to fight Mekki, but there was no telling what Badtoof would do to them if they didn't perform.

Mekki was slumped on the floor behind her, completely swamped by his oversized armour.

'It's no good just lying around,' she told him. 'We need to get out of here.'

'I am busy,' came the terse reply.

'Doing what?'

She listened and realised she could hear the sound of him tap-tap-tapping on his wrist-screen beneath all that metal.

There was a burst of static.

'What are you doing?' she repeated.

'Trying to boost my vox signal.' Mekki's rusty helmet tipped forward as he tried to nod towards the tall flagpole which rose into the air behind Badtoof, tattered banners flapping in the wind. 'That is a vox mast,' he told her. 'If I can use it to piggyback the signal...'

'You can contact the others?'

'Possibly.'

In the arena, the last biker was holding the snapping face-biter at arm's length.

'Boorrring!' Badtoof jeered, lifting a rocket launcher onto his shoulder. He pulled the trigger and the Biker-Ork exploded, drawing a huge cheer from the crowd.

The clan's 'musician' took the opportunity to take centre stage and belt out a song in praise of their warboss.

'Badtoof! Badtoof! 'Ee's tuffer than tuff.

Badtoof! Badtoof! 'Ee's gruffer than gruff.

Cross 'im and 'ee'll blast ya.

Taunt 'im and 'ee'll thump ya.

'Ee's bad. 'Ee's big.

'Ee in-no-way wears a wig.

Badtoooof!'

'We're running out of time, Mekki,' Zelia hissed, wishing she could shove her fingers in her ears.

'I am working as fast as I can,' he replied, still manipulating the vox signal. 'Talen Stormweaver. Talen Stormweaver, come in please.'

There was a crackle and Talen's distorted voice came back at them.

'Mekki? Is that you, Cog-Boy?'

'Who else would it be?' the Martian

snapped. 'Where are you?'

'Long story short, we're in a chariot being chased by a mob of angry Orks. What about you?'

'We are about to be thrown into an Ork arena to fight to the death.'

'Who? You and Zelia?'

'Yes.'

'Now that I'd pay to see.'

'Talen!' Zelia snapped. 'Are you near us?'

'How am I supposed to know that?'

'I am sending a homing pulse along this frequency,' Mekki told him. 'Can you follow it?'

'Can we?' they heard Talen ask, before replying, *'Amity says we can, if we don't get blown up first.'*

There was the sound of an explosion, and the ganger cried out.

'Talen?'

'We're okay. The Orks are throwing stink-bombs at us.' He groaned. *'And just when I thought they couldn't smell any worse.'*

In the arena, the Ork guitarist was reaching the end of his song.

'*What is* that?' Talen asked over the vox.

'Deafening!' Zelia yelled back.

She glanced over to Badtoof, who had snatched up his rocket launcher again.

'Thrasha?' he bellowed. 'You're fired!'

He pulled the trigger and the minstrel's eardrum-shredding performance came to an abrupt end.

'I wanna see some scrappin',' Badtoof hollered.

String-Guts scampered over to Zelia and Mekki's cage and yanked open the door. 'You're on! You betta make it good. You've seen wot happens when Badtoof gets bored!'

Zelia and Mekki were dragged from the cage, and thrown in front of the warboss.

'What about the homing signal?' Zelia whispered.

'I left the vox-box in the cage,' Mekki told her.

'Well?' bellowed Badtoof, his rocket launcher wavering between them. 'Wot is you waitin' for? Let battle commence!'

'How long before the others get here?' Zelia said, struggling to lift her sword.

Mekki raised his makeshift mace. 'Not soon enough,' he replied. 'We had better make this look good if we want to avoid being blown up.'

All around them the Orks started chanting: 'Fight! Fight! Fight! Fight!'

Zelia looked deep into Mekki's eyes and the Martian nodded. She took a deep breath and, with a grunt of effort, swung the razor-sharp blade of her sword towards her friend.

CHAPTER FOURTEEN

Waaagh!

'Awww, dis is dull!' Badtoof moaned. 'Dull, dull, dull.'

In front of him, Zelia and Mekki were taking it in turns to gingerly swing their weapons into each other, although none of the strikes were strong enough to cause any damage.

'Come on!' he yelled, his wig-squig desperately trying to wriggle from beneath his helmet. 'Put yer backs into it!'

He growled, becoming so frustrated that he bent his own rocket launcher in two, rendering it useless.

'Pathetic!'

'Why don't ya liven it up, boss,' String-Guts said, looking up at his leader. 'Send in bomb-squigs.'

'I've just had a brilliant idea, Worm-Guts,' Badtoof bellowed. 'Send in the bomb-squigs! Dat'll liven fings up!'

Zelia looked in horror as a gaggle of two-legged squigs scurried towards them. They were only the size of cats, but had sticks of explosives strapped to their sides. She tried to swat them away with her impossibly heavy sword, but with a maniacal cackle, the squigs hurtled themselves at the floor, blowing up where they stood. Zelia was knocked back by the first blast and tried to cover her face as more and more roaming mines detonated. Clods of charred earth and charcoaled squig-meat slapped down onto her armour.

Mekki did his best to bat away more of the giggling booby-traps, but soon another blast sent him flying. He landed on his back, unable to move.

'Awww, dis is even worse! I need mindless violence and I need it now!' Badtoof declared, thumping String-Guts for having such a stupid idea. The warboss rose to his full height and thrust his gauntleted fist into the air. 'Take 'em out, boyz. Rip and rend and do lots of uvver fings beginning with arrr!'

As one, the Tek-Hedz surged forwards. Zelia and Mekki tried to get out of the way, but could only roll around on the ground, weighed down by their armour.

They were going to be trampled alive.

Or were they?

'Wassat?' Badtoof grunted, and the Orks stopped in their tracks, tatty ears twitching.

Something was coming. They could all hear it. An inhuman roar. The thunder of giant feet.

'Is it da Biggun?' asked a slightly concussed String-Guts.

'No!' yelled a voice as a spiked chariot burst into the camp, its squig baying at the bewildered Tek-Hedz.

'Talen Stormweaver!' Mekki cheered as he spotted the ganger hanging on for dear life. Amity cracked the reins and the chariot charged around the arena.

'Is that you in there, Cog-Boy?' Talen laughed. 'What is it with you and armour?'

The Orks were all still staring, completely bamboozled by the sight of humans riding a squig-chariot.

'Is dis part of the show?' String-Guts asked.

'Of course it ain't!' Badtoof roared, turning towards his dumbfounded army. 'Wot are ya waiting for? Murderize them!'

That's when they heard the blare

of a horn and the beating of drums. Badtoof's mouth dropped open as more chariots ploughed into the arena, but this time there weren't humans at the reins.

'We brought a few friends,' Amity said, trying to keep her squig under control. 'Hope you don't mind.'

A toothy grin spread over the warboss's face. 'Don't mind? Don't mind?! Dis is brilliant! Like all me spawn-days came at once.'

'It's da Snake-Skulls, boss!' String-Guts yelled.

'I know 'oo it izz. Grab yer shootas, boyz! Dis is *Waaagh!*'

With a blistering battle cry, Badtoof charged forwards, ready to defend his camp. The rest of the warband surged with him, meeting their rivals head on.

'Where is 'ee?' Badtoof yelled, smacking a Snake-Skull Ork with his ruined rocket launcher. 'Where is dat snivelling coward Nettle-Nekk?'

The Snake-Skulls warboss replied by

leaping from his carriage, battleaxe raised and ready to cleave his enemy in two. 'Right 'ere! I'm gonna rip yer filthy 'ead from its scummy shoulders.'

'I'd like to see ya try!' Badtoof jeered, jumping up to meet him.

CHAPTER FIFTEEN

'Istory

Zelia had been on many battlefields in her life, but never like this. The sites she'd visited with her mother had witnessed battles hundreds if not thousands of years before the *Scriptor* had made planetfall. The only evidence of bloodshed were the rusty weapons and yellowed bones Zelia and her mother dug from the scorched earth. But they were just relics of the past. This was different. This wasn't history. This was happening right now, around her.

Mekki had already wriggled out of his

armour and was trying to help Zelia escape hers. Not that she wanted to. A minute ago, the Ork armour had seemed like a cage; now it was her last hope of making it through this living nightmare.

Orks battled Orks everywhere she looked. The reek of stale sweat had been replaced by the stink of gunpowder and fyceline. The clatter of axes against armour and the percussive *dakka-dakka-dakka* of shootas filled her ears, rattling her skull.

This was all her fault. She had decided to come here, choosing Weald over Pastoria. She had been so convinced that they would find her mother; so confident.

Mekki dragged her from her armour and she looked around, throwing up an arm as an explosion sent mud splattering into the air.

Talen and Amity were still in their chariot, racing towards them. Talen had some kind of bazooka which was firing missiles that encased their victims in a mass of writing weeds and the rogue trader's face was set in a mix of concentration and... what was that? Agony?

'What are they doing?' Zelia asked.

'They want us to jump on board,' Mekki replied.

'While they're moving?'

'I do not think Captain Amity knows how to stop. They have already performed three laps of the camp.'

Zelia looked at the racing chariot. She'd never make the jump, but what other choice did she have? The chariot was their only chance of escaping the battlefield.

Amity snapped the reins. Talen yelled at them to get ready. The gretchin that was snared to one of the wheels screamed. Zelia braced herself, hunkering down, waiting for the chariot to speed past.

It never made it. The wheel with the spinning gretchin came off its axle, nearly ploughing straight into Mekki. Zelia yanked him back as the chariot flipped over, throwing Talen and Amity into the air.

They tumbled and rolled, and the chariot bounced over them, still connected to its spooked squig. The red-skinned monstrosity snorted, careering towards Zelia. She froze, unable to process what was happening. This time it was Mekki who pulled her out of the way to avoid being trampled into the ground. The squig charged into the battle, mowing down Tek-Hedz and Snake-Skulls alike.

'Glad you brought us here?' Talen said, running over to them.

'Don't start,' Zelia snapped back. 'I feel bad enough already.'

'I'm joking!' he told her. 'You weren't to know the place was crawling with Orks.'

'Talen, behind you!'

Amity's cry sent the ganger spinning around. A ring-nosed Tek-Hed had been tearing towards them, axe held high.

A shot from Talen's bazooka threw the greenskin back, the bind-weed tying the berserker into a knot.

Talen shook the bazooka sadly. 'That's it. I'm out of ammo.'

'We need to get out of here,' Amity told them.

'You think? But how?'

They ducked as a bomb-squig whizzed over their heads. They were surrounded, Orks battling all around.

Zelia scanned the carnage until she saw Nettle-Nekk and Badtoof pummelling each other in the centre of the melee. Nettle-Nekk was swiping at his mortal enemy with a nail-studded club while Badtoof blocked each and every blow with his bent rocket launcher.

'Whether you were joking or not, this *is* my fault,' Zelia said. 'And I need to put it right.'

Talen looked at her as if she were mad. 'And how are you going to do that?'

'Like this,' Zelia replied, spotting the dazed bomb-squig staggering around the battlefield, clutching a boom-stick in its mouth.

Before her friends could stop her, Zelia snatched up the small creature and raced towards the battling bosses. She knew that it could go off at any minute but had to take the risk.

She thought she heard Talen call after her, but ignored him, lobbing the bomb-squig at Badtoof and Nettle-Nekk. It bounced once on the ground and landed between the two warring Orks. The squig looked up, realised that it was likely to be stomped beneath a green heel and bit down on its explosive stick.

The blast threw the two warbosses apart. Zelia didn't wait for them to get up. She raced between the fallen warriors and yelled, 'Stop!'

Charging between duelling bosses was so monumentally stupid that the warring tribes stopped fighting to gape at the small human.

'You?' Badtoof spluttered, scrambling to his feet. 'You dare knock me down? You dare strike Badtoof the Rotten?'

'I dare!' Zelia shouted back, hoping they wouldn't hear the wobble in her voice as she whirled on Nettle-Nekk. 'And I knocked you down too! The two biggest Orks on the planet and I stopped them in their tracks!'

'I'll kill ya!' Nettle-Nekk thundered.

'Will you? Tell me this – if you're so big and powerful, what does that make

me? I won, which means I'm the best.
I'm stronger than both of you, so you
better bow down.'

'You wot?'

'You heard me! Bow down!'

'To you?' Badtoof raged.

'Yes, to me. That's what Orks do, isn't
it? Winner takes all. Am I right?'

'Nah, yer wrong!' Nettle-Nekk
bellowed. 'I'll pulverise ya, ya little
squirt! I'll pound ya into da ground!'

To prove his point, he lifted his club,
ready to bring it smashing down on
Zelia's head. She gulped, realising that
her plan hadn't worked. She'd wanted
to use the Orks' own logic against
them. Instead she had just put herself
in danger.

As Nettle-Nekk's club came down, the
hulking brute suddenly looked up at
the sound of someone laughing. Zelia
yelped as his club smacked harmlessly
into the ground beside her. The
distraction had been enough to put off
his aim.

The Orks gaped at Badtoof, who was roaring with laughter, tears running down his face.

'Oi!' Nettle-Nekk yelled. 'You put me off, you guff-faced twit! Wot's so funny, anyway?'

'Dat izz!' Badtoof said, jabbing a finger at Zelia. 'Did ya hear wot she said? She's stronga dan both of us!'

He held his sides as he continued to guffaw. 'It's da funniest fing I ever 'eard.'

Nettle-Nekk looked at his rival as if he'd gone mad, before sniggering himself. The snigger turned into a snort, and the snort turned into a chortle and the chortle turned into a whoop. Before long, both Orks were hugging each other, practically falling over with laughter.

'She... said... she... woz... betta! Ha-ha-ha-haaaaa!'

In the middle of the battlefield, Talen let his useless bazooka fall to his side.

He couldn't believe what he was seeing. He'd heard people say that laughter was infectious, but the warbosses' glee had spread around both Ork tribes like a virus. All the greenskins – Tek-Hedz and Snake-Skulls alike – were howling with laughter. Warriors that had just been trying to kill each other were now slapping each other on the back as if they were old friends.

He looked around to see Mekki gaping in wonder, but frowned. Where was Amity? The captain had vanished.

From her vantage point between the warbosses, Zelia decided to press her advantage.

A minute ago, she had felt like a complete and utter failure. She had brought the *Profiteer* to the wrong planet and had almost got her friends killed. But now look at what had happened! She'd stopped a battle! Two tribes of belligerent Orks were listening to her.

All right, technically they were

laughing at her, but she had their attention nonetheless. She glanced at Talen, hoping he'd take the hint and run for the trees, but the former ganger was looking around, as if searching for something... or someone.

She had to press the advantage while she had it. She turned back to the two chiefs.

'Look at you,' Zelia said. 'A minute ago, you were at each other's throats, and now what are you doing?'

Badtoof frowned, wiping tears from his eyes. 'I dunno.'

'You're laughing, together. Laughing at me. Don't you see. All those years of fighting and battling—'

'*Waaagh!*ing,' Nettle-Nekk added.

'Yes. All those years *Waaagh!*ing. What was the point? Tell me. Why do you keep fighting?'

Badtoof shrugged his mighty shoulders. 'Sumfink to do, ain't it?'

Nettle-Nekk nodded. 'Yeah. We's Orks. We get up, we eat...'

'We belch,' Badtoof added. 'Don't forget da belching.'

'As if I could,' Nettle-Nekk acknowledged. 'And den we fight! Always 'ave done...'

'Always will,' Badtoof agreed.

'So what happens when one of you wins?' Zelia asked.

That flummoxed them. 'Wot do ya mean?' Badtoof asked.

'What happens when one of you finally beats the other?'

Badtoof scratched his wig-squig. 'Never really fort about it.'

'Yeah,' Nettle-Nekk nodded. 'We've been too busy brawlin'.'

'Then think about it now,' she implored them. 'You're all Orks. You're all the same.'

'How?' asked Nettle-Nekk.

'We're all green?' suggested Badtoof.

'Yes,' Zelia said. 'And you're all big, and you're brave, and you're... you're...'

She floundered, running out of similarities.

'You all find the same things funny,' Talen said, racing up to join them. 'Look how you all laughed at this pathetic little runt!'

'Oi,' Zelia said, beneath her breath.

'I'm helping,' Talen hissed.

'You *should* be running!'

But the warbosses were chuckling again.

'De runt *izz* funny,' said Badtoof. 'Made you laugh,' he added, nodding at Nettle-Nekk.

'And you,' the Snake-Skull chief agreed.

'See!' Zelia said. 'And if you laugh at the same things, just imagine what else you could do if you worked together.'

'Like catch the Biggun,' Talen said.

'Exactly!'

'We've been searching for 'im for ages,' Nettle-Nekk admitted.

Badtoof sniggered. 'Us too.'

Zelia couldn't believe what she was hearing. Sure, she'd started all this to try and get her friends out of danger... but what if it really worked? What if she actually got the Orks to stop their stupid war?

'Just imagine if you joined forces...' she suggested.

'You'd snare that big old squig in no time,' Talen added.

'We wud?' Nettle-Nekk asked.

'You'll go down in history,' Zelia told him. 'People will sing songs in your honour.'

'I'll sing a song for ya, boss,' String-Guts called from the sidelines, snatching up the discarded guitar-launcher.

'Not just songs,' Zelia said before the gretchin could start caterwauling. 'There will be feasts... fireworks!'

'Boom-sticks?' Nettle-Nekk asked.

'The biggest, brightest boom-sticks you could ever imagine.'

'Maybe someone will build statues of you both,' Talen said.

'I like statues,' Badtoof said. 'We've got a humongous one we use for target practice.'

Zelia and Talen exchanged a look. So that's what had blown them out of the sky – Ork missiles!

'Do you reckon our statue will be bigger?' Nettle-Nekk asked.

'I reckon so,' Badtoof agreed.

Behind them, String-Guts was starting to tune up. It sounded like a hundred grox bellowing at once.

'Wot do ya say?' Badtoof asked, holding out a sweaty hand. 'Should we do it? Should we team up?'

All eyes were on Nettle-Nekk. The Snake-Skull chief peered at the offered palm and everyone peered at him. Then, the bearded Ork clasped Badtoof's hand and pumped it furiously.

'Why not, eh? Why not?'

The Orks erupted into cheers while String-Guts struck up a rendition of *Badtoof and Nettle-Nekk, they're zogging amazing and don't ya forget it!*'

Grinning from pointed ear to pointed ear, Badtoof pulled back his hand.

'This is an 'istoric moment,

Nettle-Nekk, ol' pal,' he said, glancing down at his palm.

That's when he saw the grenade that Nettle-Nekk had slapped into his open hand.

That's when he exploded.

CHAPTER SIXTEEN

Victory

One second Badtoof was standing there, the next he was gone. All that was left of the once mighty warboss was a steaming crater and a hair-squig running for freedom.

'Zelia?'

She coughed, her throat full of dust. She had been thrown clear by the blast, the side of her face puckered from the heat.

Talen ran up, his face blackened and his tunic torn. 'Are you okay?'

He went to help her up, but she pushed him away angrily. 'You shook on it,' she shouted at Nettle-Nekk, stomping towards the chief. 'You said–'

'I said nuffink,' Nettle-Nekk sneered, picking himself up from where he had been thrown from the blast. His green skin was blackened, his face scorched, but his grin was wider than ever. 'As if Orks would ever make peace. Orks only make *Waaagh!* Right, boyz?'

Every Ork in the arena cheered, punching the air.

'But you was right about sumfink, humie,' Nettle-Nekk admitted. 'We're

betta togetha, and we *are* togetha now,
'cos I'm da biggest and I'm da best,
and EVERYONE FOLLOWS ME!'

This time the cheer was even louder,
Snake-Skulls and Tek-Hedz finally united.

'Are you wiv me, boyz?' Nettle-Nekk
called.

'Yeah!'

'I said, ARE YOU WIV ME?'

'YEAH!'

'Oo'z gonna catch da Biggun?'

'We are!'

'And wot will we do when we 'ave it?'

That stopped them. The Orks looked
at each other blankly, shuffling
uncomfortably. No greenskin could think
that far ahead – except one.

A scrawny hand went up.

'Yes?' Nettle-Nekk asked.

'Er...' stammered String-Guts, every
Orky eye on him. 'We fight the humies,
boss?'

'Exactly!' Nettle-Nekk roared. 'We fight
the humies! I likes the way ya think,
grot. Wot's yer name?'

'S-String-Guts, boss.'

'Squirm-Guts?'

The gretchin shrugged. 'Close enough.'

'Then dat is wot it will be. We'll 'ead up there,' the warboss said, pointing straight up, 'to the big fiery fings in da sky. We'll smash the humies, smash 'em good. It'll be a right dust up. The *Waaagh!* to end all *Waaaghs!'*

The Orks cheered and whooped and hit each other – not because they were enemies any more, but because they were Orks and that's just the kind of thing Orks do.

Talen swallowed. 'Do you think we've just made things worse?'

'I reckon so,' Zelia said.

'Do you think we should run away?'

'As fast as our legs can carry us.'

'Not fast enuff!' Nettle-Nekk barked, grabbing Zelia's arm and lifting her from the ground. 'We need you, humie, and yer runty friends too.'

Orks grabbed Talen and Mekki, holding them tight before they could escape.

'What are you going to do with us?' Zelia wailed, as she was dangled in front of Nettle-Nekk's face.

'Yer gonna 'elp us catch da Biggun,' he told her. 'All of us working togetha!'

'I'm sorry,' Zelia said as Weald's sun beat down on them.

'What for?' Talen asked.

'This is all my fault. Deciding to come here, trying to reason with the Orks. I was so stupid and now look at us.'

Talen pulled against the restraints that were tied around his wrists and ankles. Yes, it was fair to say that they were in trouble. The Orks had pegged them out at the foot of Emperor's Seat mountain. The knots they had tied were seemingly unbreakable and this time there wasn't any sloppy Ork war paint to use to slip free.

But Zelia blaming herself wasn't going to help anyone.

'Zelia, we haven't time for this. Yes, you said we should come here, but none of us argued, did we? We went along with it, and, if we're looking for someone to blame, which knucklehead suggested that Nettle-Nekk used bait to attract the Biggun?'

'I assume the knucklehead was you, Talen Stormweaver,' Mekki said.

'Got it in one, Cog-Boy. But we're not squig-food yet.'

Zelia didn't look like she believed him, but nodded all the same.

'So what do we do?'

That was where Talen's pep talk fell down. He had absolutely no idea what they should do next. They were on their own. Amity had vanished, and Fleapit too. He'd hoped the captain had been lying in wait, ready to rescue them when the time was right, but the odds of that happening reduced with every passing moment. It was more likely that the rogue trader had spotted an opportunity to save her own skin and grabbed it with both hands. The old Talen wouldn't have blamed her, the Talen who had learned to look out for himself in Rhal Rata's teeming undercity. But things had changed, and so had he.

That didn't mean that he knew what to do next, especially when the ground beneath them started to shake.

Boom.

It was barely noticeable at first, but soon was impossible to ignore.

Boom! Boom!

Something was coming. Something impossibly big.

Boom! Boom! Boom! BOOM!

With an ear-splitting roar, the Biggun charged out of the jungle, splintering trees in its path. There was one thing they could all agree on: the colossal squig certainly lived up to its name.

The creature was huge, blocking out the sun. It ran on two muscular legs, its body little more than a gigantic, red-skinned head. It had two rows of yellow eyes and a mouth full of teeth that could snap the *Profiteer* in two.

Steam snorted from its flat nose as it bounded forwards, heading straight for them.

Zelia screamed. Mekki screamed. Even Talen screamed. They writhed on the ground, desperately straining at their bonds, but the knots only tightened.

They were finished. There was no way to stop the colossal squig from trampling them beneath its wide, clawed feet.

Until...

A horn sounded and a thick rope

snapped up from the floor, right in front of the rampaging squig. The monster couldn't stop in time, and tripped, its bulbous body toppling forwards. It crashed head first onto the ground, and the impact reverberated around the mountainside. But that was nothing compared to its bellow as harpoons flew over its body, each trailing thick cords. These criss-crossed the fallen beast, slamming into the dirt to its left and to its right.

The squig scrambled to its feet, dragging with it the Orks who clung desperately onto their ropes, trying to anchor it in place. Other members of the now unified clans ran to their aid, grabbing ropes and hauling with all their combined might. The squig bayed, snapping at its would-be captors. It crushed them beneath its feet, slammed them against trees, but eventually was brought down, pinned to the ground by a spiderweb of ropes.

'We did it!' String-Guts cried,

guitar-launcher still around his neck. 'We captured da Biggun!'

'No, Squirm-Guts. *I* did it,' Nettle-Nekk boomed, swatting the heavy metal minstrel into a tree. 'Finally. I am victori... I am victur... I WON!'

The Orks threw back their heads and howled in triumph, banging drums and thumping each other... all except String-Guts, who picked himself up from where he had fallen, grumbling beneath his breath.

Talen saw his chance. 'Hey, String-Guts.'

The gretchin blinked. 'You got me name right.'

'Of course I did. You're String-Guts the Great.'

String-Guts looked over his shoulder to check that Talen wasn't talking about anyone else.

'I am?'

'You bet. And the way you play that instrument thing? It's amazing.'

String-Guts fiddled with the

guitar-launcher's out-of-tuning pegs. 'I 'ave been practising.'

'It shows. And I get why. You want to impress your new boss, don't you?'

String-Guts nodded furiously. 'Oh yes, more dan anything.'

'Then let us go.'

'Eh?'

'We can help each other. What did Nettle-Nekk say he wants to do?'

'Take to da fiery things in da sky.'

'To the stars, yeah, and for that he'll need a spaceship.'

'Aww, we got spaceships,' String-Guts shrugged. 'Lots of spaceships.'

'And they're all rust buckets. But what if I could take you to a spaceship that can actually fly.'

'Can actually fly?' String-Guts took a step closer. 'I'm listenin'...'

'She's called the *Profiteer* and she's amazing. The very latest weapon systems, a super-fast engine...'

'Oooh, an engine...' String-Guts parroted, his eyes sparkling.

'I could even throw in a fully working Tau battlesuit.'

'Talen!' Zelia snapped. 'What are you doing?'

'Negotiating,' Talen said.

String-Guts's face crumpled into a frown. 'Negota-wotting?'

'It means we both get something we need. You get a spaceship and we get our freedom.'

String-Guts took a step back. 'Yer freedom? I don't know about dat.'

'We need to take you to the ship, don't we?'

'*Amity*'s ship,' Zelia pointed out.

'Amity who abandoned us,' Talen responded. 'We don't owe her anything.'

'You don't owe 'er nuffink!' String-Guts corrected him.

'If you say so,' Talen said. 'You are the clever one, after all.'

String-Guts's chest puffed up. 'Yeah, I am, ain't I? So I let ye go...'

'And you get your ship.'

String-Guts let the guitar-launcher

hang around his shoulders and rubbed his hands together. 'Nettle-Nekk will be proppa pleased wiv me.'

'He'll probably make you his right-hand grot.'

String-Guts looked at his hands. 'Which one's right?'

Talen struggled to keep his temper under control, forcing himself to smile. 'The one that's not the left. So what do you say?'

String-Guts considered this for a moment and then spat into his hand and thrust his flob-covered palm towards Talen. 'I say ya got yerself a deal, humie. Shake on it.'

Talen tugged at the ropes around his wrists. 'I can't, can I?'

'Oh, yeah,' String-Guts said. 'Hang on.'

As the Orks made sure the Biggun was secured, String-Guts untied Talen's wrists. The ropes came away and his hand was free. Before the gretchin could straighten up, Talen swiped out with his hand and strummed the guitar-launcher's strings. The sudden burst of noise sent String-Guts flying back into the trees. It also nearly burst Talen's eardrums, but he didn't have time to worry about that. He was too busy freeing his other hand and feet, before tackling the knots around Zelia and Mekki's wrists.

'I thought you really meant all that for a minute,' Zelia admitted.

'Who said I didn't?' Talen said, helping her up with a wink. 'Let's go.'

They ran for the trees while the Orks were still noisily celebrating the capture of the colossal squig, but didn't get far. String-Guts sprung from the undergrowth, the barrel of his guitar-launcher pointing straight at them.

'You tricked me!' he snarled.

Talen skidded to a halt and raised his hands. 'You'd do the same to us.'

'Yer right,' the gretchin sneered. 'I would.' He called over to the Orks. 'Oi, Nettle-Nekk. The humies escaped but I catched 'em.'

The warboss turned, and saw the gretchin holding the children at guitar-point. 'So what?' he growled. 'We don't need 'em any more. You can blast 'em to smithereens for all I care.'

'Gladly,' String-Guts said, pulling back his hand to strum another deadly chord.

'No, wait,' Mekki shouted out.

'No more deals,' String-Guts said.

'It is not that,' the Martian insisted. 'Can you not hear?'

''Ear what?' the gretchin asked.

Talen knew. He couldn't just hear it, he could *feel* it. They all could. A deep shudder beneath their feet. He crouched down and squelched his hand to the muck. The ground was shaking, the tremors becoming more violent with every passing second. Then, there was the rumble, like rolling thunder. But it wasn't a storm. It was the rumble of feet. Large feet. Running feet.

Talen turned to see scaled birds flocking into the sky, a cloud of dust rising from the trees.

And then the trees were gone, trampled in the most terrifying stampede any of them had ever seen. The Biggun hadn't been alone. There was an entire herd.

CHAPTER SEVENTEEN

A Big Stink

String-Guts took one look at the stampeding squigs before throwing off his guitar-launcher and running for his life.

Unfortunately for him, the cowardly gretchin ran into the path of *another* herd of colossal squigs that were charging from the opposite direction. String-Guts squealed as a giant foot stomped down on top of him, crushing him into the dirt.

Talen scooped up the dropped guitar and ran for cover, Zelia and Mekki stumbling after him. Colossal squigs were marauding everywhere, kicking, squashing or chomping Nettle-Nekk's newly united Orks, the greenskins fighting back but horribly outnumbered.

'Over here,' Zelia yelled, running towards an overturned chariot which had been filled with grenades that were now spilled over the floor.

'Chuck 'em at the ground!' Talen said. 'Why?'

'You'll see, but you better hold your nose!'

A colossal squig was running straight

towards them. Zelia snatched up the nearest grenade and lobbed it at the monster's feet. It crunched beneath the thing's leathery sole, engulfing the squig in a thick green cloud.

'Urgh! That stinks,' Zelia said, as the smell rolled over her. Thankfully, the reek had the same effect on the squig. It roared its displeasure but turned stubby tail and ran away. Zelia grabbed more of the grenades and passed them to Mekki. 'Put them in a ring around the chariot,' she said, gagging on the foul-smelling smoke. 'They'll keep those things away.'

'So will this,' Talen yelled, strumming a sonic blast from the guitar-launcher that knocked a colossal squig and at least three Orks from their feet.

'This is all very well and good,' Mekki said, arranging the stink-mines around them, 'but we are still trapped!'

It was true. The Orks were fighting back, turning their weapons on the squigs, who in turn mashed them beneath their giant feet.

There were screams and roars and gunfire and explosions. The battle raged in all directions, cutting off any chance of escape.

Desperately, Zelia tapped her vox. 'Amity, where are you? We're in real trouble here.'

'She won't answer,' Talen said, taking out another Ork with a vibrating note.

Zelia didn't listen to him. 'Amity, we need you!'

A familiar grunting came over the vox.

'Fleapit? Is that you?'

Mekki checked his screen. 'The signal is coming from the *Profiteer*. Flegan-Pala is back on the ship.'

Zelia held the vox close to her mouth. 'Fleapit. We need your help. We're trapped and there's no sign of Amity.'

The Jokaero babbled over the vox-channel.

Zelia looked up at Mekki. 'What's he saying?'

The Martian cocked his head to listen. 'Captain Amity is there with him, on board the *Profiteer*, but...'

'But what?'

Mekki shook his head. 'He is speaking too quickly.' He spoke into his own vox. 'Flegan-Pala, slow down. What is happening?'

Zelia tapped her vox. 'Hello? Are you still there?'

Mekki frowned. 'The signal is gone. Cut off at the source.'

'So where does that leave us?'

'In trouble,' Talen yelled. 'Look!'

Zelia turned to see Nettle-Nekk charging towards them, his club held high above his head.

'I'm gonna mash you, humies! Dis izz all your fault!'

A colossal squig snapped at the warboss, but he batted the beast away with a swipe of his club.

'How do you work that out?' Talen yelled back, putting himself between the rampaging Ork and his friends.

'Yer da ones who tricked me inta trappin' da Biggun.'

The squig shook off the blow and rounded on the boss. He swept his club low, taking out the monster's legs.

'And now me Orks are gettin' battered. I wish I'd never laid eyes on ya!'

The colossal squig slammed into the ground, setting off at least three of Zelia's stink-mines.

Sickly green smoke billowed all around.

'Where is he?' Zelia cried out, her eyes stinging.

''Ere I am!' Nettle-Nekk bellowed, appearing through the sickly mist, his club swinging down. 'Time to face da music!'

'You got it!' Talen yelled, swinging the guitar-launcher around. He struck a note and a bolt of sonic energy blasted into Nettle-Nekk's chest. With a howl, the warboss was thrown back, his fake beard flipping up to cover his face. He

hit the ground, and skidded, trying to prise the stinging nettles from his now blistered skin.

'Dat really 'urts!' he wailed, pulling the nettles clear. There was a snort behind him and Nettle-Nekk twisted to see that he had landed right in front of the Biggun. The colossal squig shot forwards, bursting out of its bonds, and swallowed Nettle-Nekk with a huge, satisfied gulp.

The warboss was gone but the battle raged on, Orks and colossal squigs locked in mortal conflict. Talen spun around, planning his next move. The stink-mines had been exhausted, and the guitar-launcher's strings had all snapped.

'We're going to have to run for it,' Zelia said.

'Maybe not,' Mekki replied, raising a finger. 'Listen.'

The roar of a voidship's engines filled the air.

'It's the *Profiteer*,' Zelia exclaimed, spinning around, but her face fell.

A ship was roaring towards them, but it didn't belong to Harleen Amity.

CHAPTER EIGHTEEN

The Zealot's Heart

'Who is that?' Talen shouted above the roar of the engines.

'I don't know,' Zelia admitted.

The ship was pitch-black, with long tapered wings bristling with weapons that spat las-fire. All around them, Orks and squigs cried out as the greenskin warbuggies exploded into flames.

Zelia pushed the others down as the craft thundered low over the battle before shooting back up past the mountain. It corkscrewed in the air, looping back for another pass.

'Run!' Talen yelled, pulling her back to her feet. 'We need to get aw–'

His words were lost as light danced over his body. Zelia looked on in horror as Talen dissolved in front of her, their shocked eyes meeting before he vanished.

'W-what happened to him?' she stammered, oblivious to the carnage.

'It was a teleporter,' Mekki said, grabbing her hand and running. Zelia felt the Martian's skin tingle and looked down to see his hand glowing with the same unearthly light. In a second, Mekki was gone too.

She was on her own.

Zelia whirled around to see the mysterious spaceship launch missiles at the ground. Great clumps of earth were thrown into the air and she was blown back. She tried to get up, but her knees buckled beneath her, her legs like jelly.

Her ears ringing, Zelia crawled through the dirt. Sweat stung her eyes and she tasted blood in her mouth, but she kept going, pulling herself forwards one hand at a time.

A huge green foot slammed in front of her. She looked up to see an Ork looming over her, a ring through its nose and one eye hidden beneath a chipped wooden patch.

'I'll rip ya apart, ya little runt,' he snarled, raising a massive fist. She screamed, thrusting her face into the dirt and throwing her arms over her head.

The punch never landed.

The stink of the battlefield was gone; the mud beneath her face was gone; the heat from burning fuel, gone. Zelia opened her eyes to see nothing but dancing light. She felt as if she was floating, her body lighter than it had ever been before. She couldn't move. She couldn't speak. She couldn't even scream.

She waited until the golden glare dimmed and she felt metal beneath her cheek. She shivered. It was cold. Too cold.

She bolted up, suddenly aware that she was somewhere new. Her head spun and she fell forwards, only to be grabbed by strong hands.

'Zelia, you're okay,' Talen whispered in her ear. 'We're safe. At least, I think we are.'

There was a growl, deep and dangerous. She held onto Talen and looked around to see a large mechanical dog snarling at them, its metallic shoulders hunched and its eyes blazing red.

'Where are we?' she croaked.

'On the ship,' Mekki said, and she realised for the first time that the Martian was standing beside her.

Her stomach flipped and she thought she was going to be sick. She gagged, swallowing hard.

'You will not vomit,' came an artificial voice. She looked up to see a servo-skull hovering above the growling cyber-mastiff, its fronds twitching. 'You are on board the *Zealot's Heart*, guests of Inquisitor Jeremias.'

She gripped Talen's arm all the harder. 'Inquisitor?'

The skull floated to the left to reveal a man sitting in front of a wide viewport. He had his back to them, his hands dancing over the controls. A klaxon sounded and the servo-skull squawked in alarm.

'Incoming.'

'I see it,' the man said, with a voice like honey. He dipped the ship to the side, and a missile ripped past the viewport. 'I think I've had enough of these xenos scum.'

They swung around, the enormous statue of the Emperor lurching into view.

'Sire, you can't,' the skull said, but the inquisitor raised a gloved hand. The floating familiar fell silent.

'The greenskins have already desecrated the Emperor's image,' the man said, still not turning around. 'They will be punished.'

He pressed a button on the dashboard in front of him.

Far below, One-Eye watched as the strange ship fired on the mountain, lasers slicing into the gigantic effigy.

'LEG IT!' he yelled as the face of the mountain crashed down on top of them, burying the Orks of Weald forever.

The black ship flew through the cloud of dust that had been thrown up by the monumental rockslide and rocketed towards the stars.

On the flight deck of the inquisitor's ship, Zelia's eyes flicked down to the cyber-mastiff. The robotic animal looked as though it was about to pounce.

'Relax, Grimm,' the inquisitor instructed, finally spinning around in his chair. His uniform was as immaculate as his hair.

The hound stalked back at his

command, growling all the time.

'Good dog.' The inquisitor rose from the pilot's seat, indicating for the servo-skull to take his place. The familiar floated over to the controls, its telescopic limbs gripping levers and pressing buttons.

The man walked towards them, hands clasped behind his back. His eyes were cold, the right side of his face covered in a metal mask.

'Thank you,' Zelia said, trying to sound as if she wasn't terrified.

He waved away the gratitude. 'Please, I couldn't leave children in the clutches of those filthy animals, could I? You three have led me a merry dance, do you know that?' He stopped in front of the teleporter, looking at each of them in turn. 'A girl, a boy and a Martian.' He smiled. It wasn't reassuring. 'I heard your signal. Your cry for help.'

'We were rescued,' Talen stammered.

'So I have heard,' Jeremias replied. 'By a rogue trader.' His mouth curled into a sneer. 'Captain Harleen Amity.'

'You know her?' Zelia asked.

'Only by reputation.' He snapped his gloved fingers. A hololith of Amity's face appeared in the air beside him, holographic eyes brimming with resentment. 'She is a wanted criminal. An enemy of the Imperium.'

'She helped us,' Zelia insisted.

'Did she?'

Another click and Amity's face was replaced with a cogitator model of a very familiar coronet.

Zelia's mouth went dry.

'I see from your faces you recognise this object,' Jeremias continued. 'The Diadem of Transference. A Necron relic.'

'How do you know about that?' Zelia asked, her legs turning to jelly again.

'I have been searching for this weapon for many years.'

'Weapon?' Mekki asked.

'Yes. A weapon. One that has already caused the destruction of Targian. You have it in your possession?'

Zelia hung onto Talen. 'How did you know?'

'Do you have the Diadem?' Jeremias repeated, his tone hardening.

She looked away. 'No. It's...' Zelia sighed. 'It's on Amity's ship.'

The inquisitor's jaw tightened. 'Then we may already be too late. Harleen Amity didn't rescue you. She wanted the Diadem and now she has it, abandoning you at the first opportunity.'

'But what is she going to do with it?' Zelia asked.

Jeremias's face was grave. 'The Diadem? Sell it? Use it? I don't know. But whatever happens, the fate of the entire Imperium rests in our hands.'

'Why?' Talen asked. 'What are we going to do?'

The inquisitor smiled. 'We're going to steal it back, of course...'

GALACTIC COMPENDIUM

PART FOUR

ORKS

The most common
form of alien life in
the universe, Orks
are all brawn but
very little brain.
They live to
make war,
and will fight
anyone, including
each other. Orks

aren't born but are spawned
from fungus, and despite their tiny
nut-like brains they have a surprising

affinity for machinery. Granted, most of their machines are bolted-together rust-buckets using tech stolen from other races, but Orks don't care as long as it blows stuff up.

Fiercely tribal, Orks believe that might is always right and will naturally follow the biggest and toughest greenskin in their warband.

HOW TO SPEAK ORK

Dis = This
Da = The
Dat = That
Yer = Your
Finking = Thinking
Sumfink = Something
Scrappin' = Fighting
Enuff = Enough
Wot = What
Oo'z = Who's
Dakka = Bullets
Gob = Mouth
Lugs = Ears

Gubbinz = the inner workings of a machine

Mekboy = An Ork technician

Painboy = An Ork doctor

Stoopid = Stupid

Waaagh! = A big fight

Warboss = Leader of a clan

Wheelz = Wheeled vehicle

HOW TO COUNT LIKE AN ORK

Wun

Too

Free

Forr

Fyve

ORK WEAPONS

Big Choppa – an Ork axe, usually with extra sharp pointy bits bolted on.

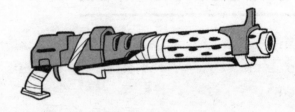

Big Shoota – an Ork cannon.

Boom-sticks – bombs

Choppas – knives. The bigger the better.

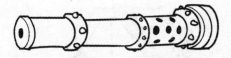

Dakkaguns – machine guns, typically found on Orkish vehicles and aircraft

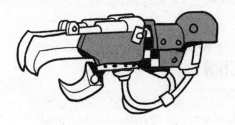

Power Fists and Power Claws – metal gauntlets to help with punching stuff. Sometimes fitted with 'shokkas', electrified knuckledusters that pack an even bigger punch.

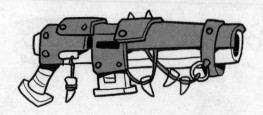

Shoota – an Ork gun, customised to make as much noise as possible.

Sluggas – Ork pistols.

GRETCHIN

Also known as grots or 'oi, you', gretchin like String-Guts are a smaller, weaker breed of Ork that basically have to do all the hard work that doesn't involve beating or blowing things up. More cowardly than their larger Ork cousins, they're sometimes sent into battle, but only as cannon fodder to draw the enemy's fire.

WHAT IS A SQUIG?

The simplest form of greenskin life, most squigs are barely more than walking mouths. Most squigs are bred for food, although there are hundreds of different varieties depending on the particular Orks' needs. Here are a few of the common types:

Attack Squigs – the most common squig of all. Bred to have razor-sharp teeth and claws, attack squigs are released to charge at the enemy, tearing apart anyone and anything in their path.

Buzzing Squigs – squigs that can fly thanks to their propeller-like tails. Will swarm on enemies to eat them alive.

Oiler Squigs – mouthless squigs that create an oily substance in their stomachs that can be squeezed out of their trunks to lubricate Ork machines.

Squiggoths – squigs the size of mammoths, large enough to carry primitive Orks into battle. These four-legged monstrosities are usually clad in heavy armour. Easily the most aggressive of all squig-life.

Squigsharks – aquatic squigs more terrifying than any Great White.

AUSPEX AND AUGURS

Auspexes are scanners used to detect energy, radiation, poisonous gases or movement. They are usually held in the hand, but are also often fitted into battle-armour, such as the helm of a Space Marine.

While auspexes only operate over a short range, the augur arrays found on voidships are far more powerful – handy for detecting enemy vessels before they attack!

GRAV-CHUTES

A grav-chute is your best chance of survival if you ever need to throw yourself out of a crashing space ship. These backpack-sized units project a suspension field that cancels out gravity so you float rather than plummet to the ground.

Two promethium-fuelled jets help regulate your descent, even offering a little directional control.

Solar-powered, a fully-charged grav-chute has enough juice to operate for an hour but will then need recharging, meaning it's always best to check before you leap.

THE IMMORTAL EMPEROR

The supreme ruler of the Imperium, the Emperor has sat on his Golden Throne for 10,000 years, his crumbling body kept alive by cybernetic devices and sheer force of will. Little is known about his life, but every day billions of humans put their trust in him to keep them safe, dedicating their lives to the wars fought in his name.

The Emperor never speaks, his will

carried out by the High Lords of Terra, twelve of the most powerful individuals in the galaxy. To speak against the Emperor is heresy and is punishable by death.

ROGUE TRADER EQUIPMENT

Rogue traders have a variety of strange and rare equipment!

Light-bringer Torches – These promethium-fuelled braziers can burn for months at a time.

Grapplewhip – A whip with claws on its tip. Handy when scaling walls. The rogue trader can lash it against any protruding ledge and then retract the flail to pull themselves up.

Lume Compass – Looting an ancient temple? Then there's no need to grope around in the dark. This spinning star can light even the darkest tomb and handily disguises itself as a brooch when not in use!

Digi-Rings – They may look like ordinary jewellery, but a rogue trader's rings can hide useful gizmos like homing signals and holo-recorders, or deadly weapons such as shock blasts or pulse grenades.

Power Cutlass – Touch a button hidden in its hilt and this power sword's blade will be bathed in crackling energy. Once activated, a power cutlass can carve through even the toughest battle-armour.

WARBIKE

Vehicle type: Ork motorbike
Weapons: dakkaguns, exhaust
(sometimes fitted with an extra smog
generator to create even more smoke)
Customisations: added skulls, spikes,
horns and studded wheels.
Rider: Biker-Ork

ABOUT THE AUTHOR

Cavan Scott has written for such popular franchises as *Star Wars, Doctor Who, Judge Dredd, LEGO DC Super Heroes, Penguins of Madagascar, Adventure Time* and many, many more. The writer of a number of novellas and short stories set within the *Warhammer 40,000* universe, including the *Warhammer Adventures: Warped Galaxies* series, Cavan became a UK number one bestseller with his 2016 World Book Day title, *Star Wars: Adventures in Wild Space – The Escape*. Find him online at www.cavanscott.com.

ABOUT THE ARTISTS

Cole Marchetti is an illustrator and concept artist from California. When he isn't sitting in front of the computer, he enjoys hiking and plein air painting. This is his first project working with Games Workshop.

Magnus Norén is a freelance illustrator and concept artist living in Sweden. His favourite subjects are fantasy and mythology, and when he isn't drawing or painting, he likes to read, watch movies and play computer games with his girlfriend.

WARPED GALAXIES

An Extract from book five
Plague of the Nurglings
by Cavan Scott
(coming late 2020)

Las-fire lanced from the *Profiteer*, striking the inquisitor's ship. Explosions blossomed across the viewscreen, the sound of the impact reverberating around the flight deck.

'Have you seen enough?'

Zelia's eyes dropped from the hololith. 'Yes,' she said quietly, and the recording of the battle fizzled out.

'The inquisitor was telling the truth,' intoned Corlak, Jeremias's loyal servo-skull as its tentacle-like mechadendrites manipulated the ship's controls. 'Captain Harleen Amity opened fire on the *Zealot's Heart*.'

'I realise this must be a shock to you,' said Inquisitor Jeremias from his high-backed command chair. He was immaculately dressed in a long coat, the mask that covered half of his face expertly polished, no doubt by Corlak. Zelia and her friends, on the other hand, were in a terrible state. Jeremias had rescued them from a battle between bloodthirsty orks and rampaging monsters, scooping them up in a teleporter beam. They were smothered head to toe in mud and ork warpaint, their smeared faces betraying the dismay they all felt. Jeremias was right – the revelation that Captain Amity had apparently abandoned them on Weald had come as a surprise. In a very short time they had come to like the rogue trader – to trust her – and for what? According to the inquisitor, she had attacked his ship as he came in to offer assistance, rocketing into the stars.

At least Jeremias looked as though he understood their disappointment, regarding them with sympathy as he idly stroked the head of his ever-present cyber-mastiff, Grimm.

'Unfortunately,' he continued, 'none of this comes as a surprise to me. Harleen Amity is wanted for numerous crimes across the Imperium.'

'Like what?' Talen snapped, his arms crossed defensively across his chest. Of all of them, the former ganger had developed the closest bond with the apparently treacherous Captain.

Jeremias shook his head. 'Where to begin?'

'You could begin with that business with the slaves, sire,' Corlak offered from the flight controls.

The inquisitor raised a gloved hand to silence the servo-skull. 'It was a rhetorical question, Corlak.' He smiled apologetically at the children. 'You'll have to forgive my familiar. He can be a little... literal.'

Mekki's brow furrowed. 'What did he mean by slaves?'

Jeremias sighed. 'It's a sad story, I'm afraid. Amity sold an entire flotilla of refugees into slavery, over four thousand people by all accounts.'

Zelia eyes widened. 'You're joking...'

'If only...' Jeremias replied. 'She had been hired to protect those poor people, and yet she betrayed them without a second thought. She lost her Warrant of Trade, of course. Her family were dishonoured and she became an outlaw.'

'Which is why she has no crew,' Zelia realised.

Jeremias raised a curious eyebrow. 'No crew?'

Zelia shook her head. 'Only a servitor...'

'Grunt,' Talen added.

Zelia shrugged. 'I always thought it

was odd, but she said that she didn't need anyone.'

The inquisitor laughed, his voice echoing around the sterile flight deck. 'More like no one wanted anything to do with her.'

'But it doesn't make sense,' Talen said. 'She saved us. Looked after us.'

'Looked after this, you mean,' Jeremias said, pressing a button on his chair's arm. A hololith glimmered into view beside him. It was the Necron Diadem that they had been trying to return to Zelia's mother, the ancient relic that had caused a Necron war-fleet to destroy Talen's home planet.

The inquisitor pointed at the artefact. 'Amity yearns for revenge. With that Diadem she could destroy any planet under the Emperor's protection. That is what she and her accomplice wanted all along.'

'Her what?' Zelia asked. Surely he didn't mean Grunt?

'Her inside man. Or should I say...
Jokaero.'

Now it was Mekki's turn to
look amazed. 'You can't mean...
Flegan-Pala...?'